Ranger's Homecoming

The Rescue Rangers Book 2

Caitlyn Lynch

Shenanigans Press

Paperback Edition

Contents

1. Chapter One 1
2. Chapter Two 20
3. Chapter Three 36
4. Chapter Four 48
5. Chapter Five 63
6. Chapter Six 77
7. Chapter Seven 90
8. Chapter Eight 103
9. Chapter Nine 116
10. Chapter Ten 132
11. Chapter Eleven 151
12. Chapter Twelve 165

13. Chapter Thirteen 180

14. Chapter Fourteen 198

15. Chapter Fifteen 214

16. Chapter Sixteen 227

17. Chapter Seventeen 242

18. Chapter Eighteen 264

19. Chapter Nineteen 280

20. Chapter Twenty 294

21. Chapter Twenty-One 311

Epilogue 317

Also By Caitlyn Lynch 324

Chapter One

The first raindrop fell in a thick splatter on the windshield, and Jason Hunter cursed softly to himself. He'd hoped to get to Woodvale before the storm broke, but he was still a ways out. He probably shouldn't have stopped to grab coffee, but it was a long drive from Spokane to the far north of Idaho and the boredom had got to him. That and the terrible country music station which was all the cheap radio in his hire car would pick up.

Sighing, he turned the wipers on and hoped the rain wouldn't get too heavy. He was in the thick woods to the west and south of the town now, knew that foul weather could easily bring one of the huge pines bordering the road crashing down to block his path. At least, this late in the year it was unlikely to snow; he'd seen snow here in April plenty of times growing up, but the weather forecasts he'd heard on the radio had only predicted rain.

Darkness was falling fast, exacerbated by the looming storm clouds and the tall, dark trees. The raindrops beginning to fall in ever greater numbers made switching the headlights on an absolute necessity. Flicking the switch, Jason pushed a little harder on the gas, edging up over the speed limit. He'd barely seen another vehicle in the last half hour, doubted there would be any authorities up here to pull him over for speeding anyway.

The sign for Woodvale appeared in the lights like a welcoming beacon. Smiling, Jason eased off the gas and turned off I-95 with a sense of relief, knowing there were less than ten miles left to go. Just a few more minutes and he'd be in Aunt Rose's comfortable little house, the only place he'd ever really thought of as home.

A flicker of movement to his left caught his attention. He turned his head, taking his foot off the gas to hover over the brake pedal. A deer or an elk choosing this moment to bound across the road could ruin his whole day; the cheap little rental car would be totaled in a heavy collision.

It wasn't a deer. It was a person, white hair catching the light as they stumbled out of the forest and onto the road, right into his path. Jason slammed on the brakes and swerved, barely missing the pedestrian as the car skidded on the wet road. He swore loudly and steered into the skid, finally regaining control and screeching to a halt.

"What the hell?" Jason said aloud, before getting out of the car and looking back along the road. All he could see was what looked like a bundle of rags, collapsed right on the dividing line between the two lanes. Had he hit the person, after all? He ran to the bundle, fell to his knees.

"Are you all right?" he asked, feeling stupid; reaching out, he laid a hand on what felt suddenly like a very fragile form, feeling towards the neck for a pulse. "Did I hit you?"

In the dim red glow from the car's rear lights he couldn't see well, couldn't assess their condition. Not until the person rolled towards him and an aged, female face looked up at him, a cracked voice whispering;

“Help me. Please help me!”

“What the actual fuck,” Jason said as the old lady’s eyes closed, but it was more of a statement than a question. Looking around, he had to wonder where the hell she’d come from; as far as he knew there were no houses in this area, or there never had been when he lived there. These woods were part of the giant timber stands that gave Woodvale its name and fed the local logging industry with a constant supply of quality timber.

He couldn’t see that he had a lot of choice. The woman was barely conscious, whimpering slightly as he quickly passed his hands over her limbs, checking for breaks.

“Can you tell me your name?” Jason asked urgently, carefully lifting her into his arms. He’d have to put her on the back seat of the car. She was a small woman, fragile;

he reckoned she probably weighed no more than seventy pounds, nothing to a soldier who was used to carrying a combat load a good deal heavier than that for days at a time.

“Julia,” she croaked out, before suddenly starting to struggle. “The dogs! I can hear the dogs!”

Startled, Jason listened, but couldn’t hear anything. “I can’t hear any dogs, okay? I’m gonna put you in my car, get you to the hospital.” He opened the car door and laid her carefully on the back seat. In the meager light cast by the car’s internal bulb, he saw for the first time how strange her appearance was.

Julia was wearing what appeared to be army fatigue pants, woodland pattern, several sizes too big for her, and a similarly large olive-green T-shirt. Heavy boots on her feet were thickly clogged with mud.

She had to be at least eighty years old.

“What the hell is going on here? Who are you?” Jason asked in utter puzzlement, but she appeared to have fainted as soon as her head hit the seat. He checked her pulse — slow, but strong — and took off his jacket to cover her. She was wet through and freezing cold.

Checking the trunk, he found a travel blanket and added that on top of Julia as well. The best thing he could do for her was drive her into town as quickly as possible, get her to the small medical clinic that was all Woodvale boasted. At least Julia could get medical treatment there, and if it was serious, maybe she could be airlifted to a bigger hospital.

Thinking ahead, he realized he should call it in, arrange for the clinic's medical staff to meet him. Getting back into the driver's seat, he rummaged in the duffel bag he'd thrown into the footwell on the other side, looking for his cellphone.

"No signal. Shit!" Glancing back at Julia, he grimaced before concluding he should drive on until he got a signal and then stop to make the call. It would still save time if he could get the medical staff to meet him at the clinic. Starting the car, he set off again into the increasingly heavy rain.

"You with me, Julia?" Jason called back when he sensed movement behind him. "Can you speak to me?"

"The dogs," came a faint, terrified whimper from the back seat.

"There aren't any dogs. I'm taking you to hospital. Can you tell me your surname, Julia?"

She didn't answer him; he adjusted the mirror to check on her, saw that her eyes were closed. She was shuddering, great tremors that wracked her slight frame.

"Not long now," he promised, glanced down at where his phone rested on the passenger seat and saw gratefully that there was a bar of signal. "I'm gonna stop and call ahead, tell them we're coming in. We'll be off again in a minute."

She didn't respond, but then he didn't really expect her to. If he'd ever known the numbers for the Woodvale medical clinic or police station, he'd long since forgotten them, so he just dialled 911.

"Woodvale emergency services, what is the nature of your emergency?" a bored-sounding female voice answered after a couple of rings.

"I've picked up an injured woman who was wandering around in the woods outside of town. I'm bringing her in to the medical clinic, hoping you can get the staff to meet me there."

The dispatcher's voice sharpened. "I can arrange that. What are the nature of her injuries?"

"I don't exactly know," Jason admitted, "but she's an old lady, soaked through and exhausted. She's oddly dressed and seems emaciated."

There was a momentary silence; he guessed he was on hold while the dispatcher relayed the information. She came back on the line a few seconds later.

"Thank you. Is she conscious?"

"Not at the moment, but she has been briefly. Told me her name was Julia."

“Julia?” It was definitely an exclamation. “Julia Bulridge?”

“I didn’t get her surname, I’m sorry. She’s not coherent.”

“And who exactly are you?” There was a distinct tone of suspicion in the voice now, but Jason figured he had nothing to hide.

“Jason Hunter.”

There was another momentary silence, and then another voice came on the line, a man’s voice this time. Jason had to strain to hear; the rain was coming down really hard now, hammering on the car’s roof. He covered his other ear with his hand.

“Please repeat that?”

“You one of THE Hunter family?”

“I fail to see how that’s important right now,” Jason snapped. “Just have the medical staff meet me at the clinic.” Hanging up, he restarted the engine. “Hang in there, Julia. Not long now.” Instinctively, he glanced in the mirror again... and froze.

The back seat was empty.

"Julia?" Shocked, he twisted around. The rear door was open on the passenger side; she must have opened it and got out while he had his ear covered, speaking to the dispatcher. "What the ever-loving fuck..." This entire episode was getting ever more bizarre. Still, he couldn't leave her out here in the middle of nowhere, not in this storm and the state she'd been in. Shutting off the engine again, he grabbed his phone and switched on the built-in flashlight. It was damn dark out there now.

"Julia!" Jason cast the light around, peering into the darkness. "Julia, it's okay! I just want to help you!"

There was no sound but for the rain, pouring down heavily and soaking him to the skin in moments. He called a few more times, but if she'd gone into the trees and didn't want to be found, he had no hope of finding her, not alone as he was with the scant light from his phone. Glancing into the backseat, he saw she'd left the blanket but taken his jacket.

Irresolute for a minute, he closed the rear door and got back into the car, started the engine yet again. The dispatcher seemed to know who Julia was; it was possible she pulled this kind of stunt regularly. At any rate, heading for the police station to report what had happened in person and organize some properly equipped help seemed like the best idea right now, and he was only a few minutes out of town.

The police station and medical clinic were right next to each other directly across from city hall, just as Jason remembered it. The medical clinic was dark, but welcoming lights and an open door beckoned him into the police station.

The storm had passed and the rain was slowing; parking the car, Jason grabbed his duffel bag and headed into the station. A grizzled, older man wearing a sergeant's uniform looked up at him wearily from the front desk.

"Can I help you?"

"My name's Jason Hunter, I called in a few minutes ago about finding an old lady injured out in the woods."

"Julia Bulridge?" The man stood, looking suddenly a lot less weary. "Where is she?"

"I don't know if she's Julia Bulridge or not, just that her name is Julia. And I don't know where she is either, I'm afraid. She took off into the woods again."

The sergeant pointed a gnarled finger. "That her?"

Jason turned to see a large color poster up on the wall opposite the desk.

HAVE YOU SEEN THIS WOMAN?

It was definitely a photo of Julia, though in the image she looked healthy and smiling, and the information underneath stated that she'd been missing for a little over a week.

"Yes, that's her!" Startled, Jason turned back to the sergeant. "I'd not long turned off the I-95 when she came stumbling out of the woods. I nearly ran over her. She was in a pretty bad way."

"But she ran off again, and you couldn't catch her?" The sergeant's eyes traveled over Jason incredulously. With his black T-shirt soaked and clinging to his upper body, his powerful physique was quite evident, he realized.

"She must have taken off while I was on the phone with the dispatcher," Jason admitted, aware that it sounded pretty feeble. "Look, I have no reason to lie to you. I got back out of the car and yelled for her, looked around, but she'd taken off into the woods. The rain had started and it's pretty dark out there. I didn't have a torch, couldn't search for her effectively, not if she was trying to hide for some reason. I figured the best thing to do was to come back to town and organize a properly equipped search party."

"Very wise, Mr Hunter," another voice said, and Jason looked around to see that the door at the end of the counter had opened silently and a man was standing there, watching him. The star on his breast pocket gave away his identity.

"Sheriff," Jason tipped his head politely.

"I think you'd better come on through and tell me everything. Julia Bulridge's disappearance is considered a criminal case."

"I can do that, no problem, but can you start organizing the search party first? I can show you where I was when she got out of the car..."

The desk sergeant slapped a map on the desk and handed Jason a pencil; he took only a few seconds to orient himself before marking an X on the map.

"There. Less than a mile from the I-95 turnoff, within a hundred yards of where the road bends around Copper Mountain."

"Sure of that, are you?" the sheriff asked, his tone cynical.

"I grew up here in Woodvale, Sheriff. I'm sure."

"All right. See to it, Barker." The sheriff nodded at the sergeant and gestured Jason to follow him.

Jason found himself in the sheriff's office, discovered the man's name from the engraved brass nameplate on his desk. Sheriff Thomas McCarthy. Jason wracked his brain but couldn't remember any McCarthys in Woodvale; the man was around forty by his estimation, fairly young for a sheriff here. He carried himself with an air of quiet competence Jason certainly recognized; he'd seen it every day for many years now.

"You're former military, Sheriff McCarthy?" he asked politely, looking around the room. There weren't any photographs on the walls, just the mounted heads of stuffed animals and an ugly painting of a dead stag with wolves tearing at its throat. It was hardly a reassuring image, and Jason hoped the sheriff didn't make a habit of questioning witnesses in here.

"What makes you ask?"

"You've got the bearing, that's all," Jason shrugged, wondering why the man might be touchy about his service. "Just bein' neighborly."

"Navy," McCarthy said finally, taking a seat behind the desk and gesturing Jason to sit down.

"You're a long way from the ocean."

"And you're a long way from Atlanta, Lieutenant Hunter. What brings you to Woodvale?"

Jason stiffened slightly. "If you know my former rank," he stressed the word, "then you know I was born and raised here. My Aunt Rose is ill. I'm here to see her."

"Former? You're no longer with the Rangers?" McCarthy jumped at the information.

"That's correct. My term was up four months ago and I was offered a very lucrative position by my former captain, recently retired from the service himself. I accepted."

"In Atlanta?" The sheriff looked at his computer screen, angled away from Jason. He was willing to bet that at least the declassified portion of his service record was displayed there, wondered what strings the man had pulled to get that so fast. He reckoned it had been no more than twenty minutes since he'd told the dispatcher his name.

"In Guàlize, actually."

McCarthy blinked at that, stared at him. "Guàlize?"

Jason shrugged. "My former captain in the Rangers married the President-elect's daughter. He's working for the Guàlizean government, training a squad of crack troops for anti-narcotics operations. He asked me to go down there to work with them, and I accepted the job offer. Like I said, the money's good."

"So you've been living in Guàlize... for how long?"

"Four months."

"I see." Picking up a pen, McCarthy flipped open a notebook and scribbled something. Jason gritted his teeth.

"Are we done here? Because if we are, I'd like to go back out and join the search for Julia."

"I don't think so, Mr Hunter." McCarthy gave him a glacial stare. "You've been away a long time. Leave the search to folks who know the area as it is now. We'll find Mrs Bulridge, if she's out there."

For a moment there was a silent staring match between the two men, a battle of wills, and then Jason sighed and stood up.

"I'm just here to visit my aunt, Sheriff. I hope you find Mrs Bulridge." It wasn't worth pissing the man off, angry though he felt at McCarthy's obvious obstructionism.

"How long are you planning to stay in Woodvale?" the sheriff asked, rising and following Jason as he left the office.

"I don't know yet," Jason answered honestly. "My aunt is very ill. Dying. I have clearance from my employers to stay as long as I need."

"I see." The sheriff looked thoroughly displeased at that news. "Well. Don't leave town without letting us know, Mr Hunter. You're a witness, after all."

Jason gritted his teeth and nodded silently. McCarthy just rubbed him the wrong way, that was all, he tried to tell himself. The police station which had been quiet earlier was a hive of activity now, maps being spread over desks and men equipped with sturdy outdoor gear and big torches coming in. The sheriff stepped forward to take comment of the operation, but his eyes never left Jason as the former soldier departed the scene.

Getting back into his rental car, Jason took a deep breath and tried to let his anger go. He wanted badly to be a part of the search efforts, but the sheriff had just flatly told him to stay away, and going out there on his own would be futile, quite probably leading to him getting arrested. Clenching his hands on the wheel, he shook his head in frustration. McCarthy was right about one thing though, in that it had been a very long time since Jason wandered these woods. There were plenty of capable men in that police station, and in her weakened state, Julia couldn't have gone far. They'd find her — if she was still alive.

Starting the car, Jason determined to come back to the police station in the morning. Right now, Aunt Rose was waiting for him.

Chapter Two

Aunt Rose's house was unlit when he pulled up outside. Frowning, Jason glanced next door, saw plenty of lights on at her neighbor's house. The Barclays had lived there since he was a child, and it was Mrs Barclay who had called to let him know just how ill Aunt Rose was.

"Jason Hunter, aren't you a sight for sore eyes," Mr Barclay greeted him as he opened the door to Jason's knock. "Come in, come in."

Shocked by how much the man had aged, Jason realized with a twitch of guilt that it had been nearly ten years since he last set foot in Woodvale. Aunt Rose had always come to him, flying down to Atlanta to visit at least once a year at Jason's expense, a bill he was more than happy to foot.

"Good to see you, sir." He shook Mr Barclay's hand. "Ma'am. Please don't get up." Mrs Barclay had aged too; while he remembered a smiling motherly woman in her late middle years, she was now definitely into old age, her hair blue-rinsed white and her capable hands gnarled and delicate. He went over to where she sat in a comfortable armchair, a quilt over her lap, and impulsively bent down to kiss her cheek.

"It's good to see you too, Jason." She smiled up at him. "But I'm afraid your aunt isn't feeling well this evening. I stopped in to see her earlier, took her a bite of dinner... she managed to eat a little of it, but wanted to go to bed early. I didn't tell her you were coming, as you asked."

"I won't disturb her tonight, then," Jason said immediately. "I can get a room at the motel, come see her in the morning."

"You could stay here, the couch pulls out..."

"I wouldn't dream of it. Thank you for the offer, truly, but you've already done so much for Aunt Rose. I wouldn't even know she was ill if it wasn't for you."

Rose hadn't let on to Jason when her doctor told her that her increasingly troubling stomach pains were because of an inoperable, slow-growing cancer. It was Mrs Barclay who had written to him, telling him that Rose's insurance was insufficient to cover her medical bills, and she was considering selling her house. He'd been on deployment in Afghanistan when the letter arrived, unable to return home, but he'd immediately called Rose and told her to stop worrying about the bills.

"Rose has been a good friend all these years." Mr Barclay gruffly waved away his thanks. "You're more than welcome to stay," and then as Jason shook his head, "well, at least have a bite to eat? Emma made a pot roast and there are plenty of leftovers."

His stomach growled at the mere thought, reminding him it had been a long time since lunch, and Mrs Barclay laughed. "Go sit down and I'll dish you some up. I remember your appetite all too well, young man."

“I’m not a growing teenager any more!” Jason chuckled, but he allowed them to urge him to the table. Soon there was a heaping plate in front of him, a glass of juice at his elbow. The Barclays made themselves tea and sat down to keep him company. He answered questions about his work in Guàlize in between bites, and when they seemed to run out of questions, took the opportunity to ask;

“What can you tell me about the disappearance of Julia Bulridge?”

They both looked startled. “Where did you hear about that?” Mr Barclay asked.

So, of course, Jason had to tell them about his encounter with the old lady on the road. At least they didn’t doubt it had actually happened, he thought wryly as they reacted with shock, pelting him with questions. At last, he was able to ask his original question again.

“The sheriff told me that her disappearance is being treated as a criminal case. Why is that?”

"Because she's the sixth person to go missing from Woodvale in five months," Mr Barclay said flatly.

"What?" Shocked, Jason rocked back in his chair.

"Bill, you're exaggerating things," Mrs Barclay chided, shaking her head. "It's not like that, Jason. Really, she's the third. The first one was old Mr Ellis, you might remember him? His family own the hardware store, he used to run it."

Jason nodded, his mouth full. He'd worked a part-time job for Ellis during high school, stacking shelves and hauling crates. The old man had been firm but decent, paying a fair wage and even dishing out a nice Christmas bonus.

"He developed dementia a couple years back, the poor soul. He was living with his son and daughter-in-law, but they both work in the store so it wasn't so easy to keep an eye on him. He started wandering, and one day he just wandered off into the woods and never came back."

"Nothing mysterious about that," Jason swallowed before saying. "Tragic, but it happens."

"And it happened exactly the same way not three weeks later, to Jenny Moreau, a young woman with Down's Syndrome. She was in the woods picking mushrooms with her brother and he lost her. No trace found."

That was a bit weirder. Jason set down his fork. "A proper search was done?"

"Dogs brought in and everything." Mr Barclay nodded sagely. "A lot of people pointed fingers at the Moreau boy; he's her sole carer and it can't have been easy, but I know that boy. He adored his sister, and he'd never hurt a hair on her head. Used to get into fights over her at school, looking out for her."

Mr Barclay had been a teacher at the high school, had taught science and math, Jason remembered. He nodded slowly, remembering how good a judge of character the older man had always been.

"So what about the other three disappearances?" he asked. "Since you said that Julia Bulridge was really only the third, and those other two sound reasonably legitimate to me."

"Three teenagers," Mrs Barclay said, "the two Whitton boys, and a no-good kid called Mark Martin. They just ran off, if you ask me." She shook her head. "I don't think you could call their disappearance suspicious. They stole a car!"

"Yes, but what you're missing out is that Mark Martin is Julia Bulridge's grandson," Mr Barclay disagreed with her, "and she kicked up quite a stink, insisting that he'd never disappear without a word to her. Her son-in-law's a worthless twit and her daughter's stoned out of her mind half the time," he told Jason, his expression disapproving, "so it's no surprise that Mark's not exactly a model citizen. That boy loved his grandmother, though, and I don't think he really would disappear with not a word to her for three whole months. Not even a phone call."

Jason sipped his juice thoughtfully, considering what he'd been told. "It does sound pretty odd," he said finally. "And Julia kicked up a stink about it?"

"That's right. Insisted that he be classified as a missing person and that it was a criminal case. She was in the sheriff's office every day berating him and demanding that the police keep searching. Until she disappeared, too. She asked too many questions, I'm telling you." Mr Barclay sat back with a decisive nod.

"Your imagination's too active," Mrs Barclay snorted, nudging him. "I told you, she heard from Mark and went to look for him!"

"And I almost thought you might be right, right up until Jason here turned up and told us about seeing her out in the woods in a dreadful state."

There wasn't really much Mrs Barclay could say to that. She picked up her teacup and drank, a worried expression on her face. Her husband nodded, more sorrowfully than triumphantly, and turned back to Jason.

"Julia's disappearance is being treated as a criminal case mainly because there's money involved. She was quite well-off, and her son-in-law is trying to get his hands on her assets."

"Which makes him look extremely suspicious," Jason realized.

"He's the prime suspect. Personally, I don't think he'd have the initiative to think up a plan to get rid of Julia," Mr Barclay shook his head. "What kind of an idiot would throw suspicion on himself straight away by trying to access her bank accounts once it was clear she was missing, anyway? Even Tom Martin isn't that dense."

"I was at school with a Tom Martin," Jason said, "he was a year older than me." He remembered a big kid, not too bright but good at sports, popular. He'd been a linebacker on the school football team when Jason was quarterback.

"That's the boy. Did badly at school and hasn't done much since. Knocked up the Bulridge girl barely a few weeks after the family moved to town." Mr Barclay shook his head. "It's a shame. She was only seventeen, a bright girl, but she never came back to school to graduate after she had the baby. Got into drugs to cope. Such a waste."

There wasn't much Jason could do but agree. He thanked the Barclays for their hospitality, once again declined their offer of the pull-out couch, and headed back out. The motel was only a block away, so he left the rental car parked outside his aunt's house and walked. The rain had stopped entirely now, the night air clear and fresh, the scent of wet pine trees overlaying everything. He breathed deep, savoring the familiar background scent. He'd missed it, he realized as he walked down the street with long, loose strides. The smell of wet pine trees would always somehow be the scent of home.

A bored night clerk issued him a room key in exchange for a swipe of his credit card, and Jason let himself into the issued room. A glance around told him that it was pretty much like every other motel room he'd ever been in; bland and soulless, though cleaner than plenty he'd inhabited over the years. Taking a shower, he settled into bed and turned on the small television, wondering if there'd be anything on the news about the hunt for Julia, but a quick flick through the channels found nothing.

It took him a long while to fall asleep, thinking about the strange disappearances in Woodvale. Dreams of Julia's terror haunted him, the fearful way she'd cried out about dogs.

Dogs. Jason's subconscious latched onto that, and suddenly he was wide awake and staring at the ceiling. Julia thought she was being hunted by dogs. He hadn't heard any dogs out there in the woods, but that didn't mean much, not with the storm going on.

Jason wasn't sure what was so important about the thought, but he'd learned to trust his intuition; it had saved his neck more than once during his military career. He made a mental note to ask about dogs in the woods when he talked to Mr Barclay again as sleep finally claimed him.

A pale gray light was beginning to filter through the motel room's thin curtain. With a sigh Jason sat up, swinging his legs over the edge of the bed. He was too used to early starts to sleep in. Too early to go over to Aunt Rose's or to talk to the Barclays again, but maybe he'd walk over to the diner and get some breakfast, listen in on a few conversations. Folks there would surely be talking about the search for Julia even if it wasn't on the TV news.

The diner was a warm, brightly welcoming beacon in the dull morning, already crowded with folks hunched over their pancakes and bacon. Nobody stopped talking when Jason came in; a couple of folks turned to look at him but he got no other reaction apart from a couple of curious looks, the same kind any stranger walking into a small-town diner might get.

A harried waitress waved him to choose a table; he picked a booth towards the back where he could sit and see most of the room. Nodding pleasantly to the waitress as she plonked a mug on the table and filled it with steaming black coffee, he said;

"Keep that stuff comin', please."

"Sure thing, hon." She was a few years older than him, he thought; she had a nice smile and a name tag that said Lulu. "Breakfast?" A plastic-coated menu was slapped down on the table when he nodded, and she bustled off to top up someone else's coffee. Jason sipped on his and watched the room quietly, listening in to the chatter.

Just as he'd suspected, Julia was the primary topic of conversation in the room, everyone talking about his sighting of her last night and the search party who were apparently still out in the woods. His name didn't come up, though, which made him wonder who the source of the rumors was. Not the sheriff, the desk sergeant or the dispatcher, all of whom knew his name.

Jason was quietly tucking into his scrambled eggs, link sausage and wholewheat toast when the door swung open and the sheriff entered, flanked by two uniformed deputies. McCarthy looked across the room and their eyes met as silence fell.

Uh-oh, Jason thought as the three officers headed for him in lockstep. Setting his fork down and taking a sip of his coffee, he smiled pleasantly as the police officers stopped in front of his booth.

"Good morning, Sheriff."

"I don't know what the fuck you think you're playing at," McCarthy snapped, his face contorted in an ugly scowl, “but you’re coming with us.”

Jason blinked, and reached into his pocket. The two deputies reacted by reaching for their guns.

“Easy, boys,” he said quietly, bringing his hand back into view and placing both of them on the table. “I’m not armed. I’m just gettin’ out my wallet. Haven’t paid for my breakfast yet, and I’m sure not gonna stiff Lulu on her tip. She’s earned it.”

“Pay for your goddamn breakfast and let’s go,” McCarthy snapped. Jason pulled out his wallet, nice and slow, and withdrew a couple of twenties; over three times the cost of his breakfast. He trapped the bills under his coffee cup with a nod to Lulu, who was watching the proceedings with wide eyes.

“Have you found Mrs Bulridge?” Jason asked it loudly as he rose to his feet, knowing it was the question everyone wanted to know the answer to. A murmur around the diner made the sheriff glance around.

“Yes, Mr Hunter, we have. We found her dead. In your aunt’s back garden.”

"Oh, wow, this doesn't look like a setup at all," Jason said dryly with a roll of his eyes, which seemed to make McCarthy hesitate only briefly.

"If that's your defense, the DA is gonna love you," he snapped. "Jason Hunter, you are under arrest for the murder of Julia Bulridge. Turn around and put your hands behind your back."

Jason wasn't particularly keen on the idea of being escorted out of the diner in handcuffs, but he was even less keen on being shot 'resisting arrest'. So, he calmly turned his back and offered his wrists up to be cuffed while the sheriff read him his rights.

"I want a lawyer," he said clearly and loudly, for the benefit of the whole room, "and I reserve the right to remain silent until I am appointed competent legal counsel." His eyes met Lulu's. She looked at the pair of twenties under his coffee cup and nodded; as the police escorted him out, he saw from the corner of his eye that she fished a cell phone from her apron pocket.

She’d definitely earned that tip. And the fact she was -- hopefully -- calling a lawyer for him, a total stranger, told him something else.

The town wasn’t fond of Sheriff McCarthy.

Chapter Three

Carla Ramirez was two miles into the three mile run she made herself slog through at least twice a week when the phone in her jacket pocket rang. For a brief moment, she considered running on, but she was exhausted anyway. She slowed to a walk, but kept her feet moving, not wanting to stiffen up. It was cold, and if she wasn't going to run home, she still needed to maintain a brisk pace.

Fishing her phone out of her pocket, she jabbed at the screen with cold fingers clammy with sweat, cursing under her breath until the touchscreen acknowledged her and unlocked, answering the call. It wasn't a number she recognized, but that was hardly unusual; her number was publicly available. On her website, just to start with.

“Attorney at law Carla Ramirez speaking,” she said, trying to sound crisp but aware she was just coming off breathless.

“It’s Lulu Jones, Miz Ramirez,” a voice with several thousand cigarettes in its past said.

“Lulu.” Carla didn’t stop walking, but she did roll her eyes. “Harry get himself into strife again?”

“No, he’s doing good. Holding down his job at the feed store. But I just saw somethin’ real weird happen at the diner. Didja hear yet that they found Julia Bulridge’s body?”

Carla’s legs stopped working, and she almost stumbled, pausing to put her hand against the fence of a house she was passing. “I didn’t.”

“In the garden at old Mrs Hunter’s house, apparently. But the weird thing is, her nephew’s back in town, and they’re saying he killed Julia. The sheriff just arrested him.”

“Right.” Carla didn’t see how that was of any interest to her. The Hunter family was trouble she didn't want to touch. Too much money, too much power. She remembered the nephew, had been at school with him. He'd been a popular jock type, but had left town to join the military, as she vaguely recalled. "Sorry, Lulu… why are you calling me?"

"'Cause the Hunter boy, he said he's bein' framed. Said loudly as they were puttin' the cuffs on that he wasn't talkin' and he wanted a lawyer. Looked me right in the eyes and left me a hefty tip. Didn't know what to do except call you, Miz Ramirez. Thought maybe you could go down the station and maybe help him out."

This didn't make any sense. Lulu had no love for the Hunters; Philip Hunter, the man who owned half the town, had hired and fired just about every member of Lulu's family at some point, including her son Harry, who had tried and failed to get his own back with a little bit of improvisational arson at one of Philip Hunter's properties. It hadn't gone well. Harry had served three years at the state's pleasure at Cottonwood.

“Why would a Hunter need me?” she asked, puzzled. “Philip will have his high-priced big city lawyers here by mid-morning. Even if his nephew murdered Julia Bulridge, they’ll no doubt be able to manage to get him off scot-free.”

She was nearly home, sweat drying fast on her chilled skin, thinking longingly of a hot shower and some even hotter coffee before she plunged into the stack of paperwork on her desk.

“He asked for a lawyer, Miz Ramirez,” Lulu said stubbornly. “And you know how the sheriff’s in Philip Hunter’s pocket? He looked right pleased to be putting cuffs on that boy.”

Now that really didn’t make sense. Carla sighed, and instead of heading upstairs to the bathroom after opening the front door, she picked up her car keys. She’d go down to the police station and just check up on things. Make sure proper procedure was being followed.

This time around, Jason didn't get escorted into the sheriff's taxidermy-haven office, but into a barren little interrogation room. Shoved to sit down on a hard metal chair firmly bolted to the floor, they left his hands cuffed behind him. The sheriff took a seat and the other two stood in the corners of the room and tried to look intimidating.

Jason really wasn't impressed. He sat at his ease, perfectly used to having his back held straight and hands behind his back. It was just a seated version of parade rest, that was all. Sheriff McCarthy tried to stare him down, but better men than he had failed with that tactic. Jason let his gaze go to a thousand-yard-stare and waited. It didn't take long.

"Why did you kill Julia Bulridge?" McCarthy led out with.

Jason rolled his eyes. "We both know I didn't do any such thing. Where's my phone call? I want a lawyer."

"You'll get a phone call when I damn well say so!"

“Are you even recording this?” Jason looked pointedly around the room, staring into the upper corners. “Is that camera even on?”

“It’s on.” McCarthy visibly ground his teeth.

“Well, that’s something at least. Means you can’t beat the shit out of me and claim I was resisting arrest.”

For a moment he thought McCarthy was actually going to lose his temper and punch him anyway; the man put both hands on the table and half-shoved himself to his feet, his face purpling with rage.

One of the deputies let out a very unsubtle cough and McCarthy hesitated before dropping back into his seat, breathing hard.

“You’re going to regret ever coming back to Woodvale, Jason Hunter,” he growled.

“I already do, and I didn’t even get to see my aunt yet.”

McCarthy blinked at that, frowned, and opened his mouth; he was interrupted by a sharp rapping on the mirror-glass window on one wall of the room. Frowning, he looked up at it and shook his head.

"Go see what that is. I'm in the middle of a goddamn interrogation here..."

The moment the deputy opened the door, it was shoved wide and a tiny fireball of a woman erupted in.

"You are not in the middle of an interrogation, Sheriff McCarthy, because my client already informed you that he would be exercising his right to remain silent until his lawyer was present. Well, I'm here, and you can get those cuffs off and get the hell out!"

Grinning, Jason watched as the tiny woman berated the sheriff, demanding that they be moved to a private room where she could talk to him in confidence, ordering the deputies to take the cuffs off.

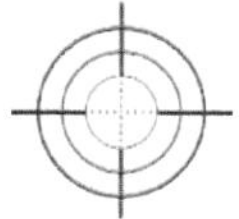

"On your head be it, Carla," McCarthy snapped, his face beet-red with frustration and rage, "if he snaps your neck like he did to poor Julia Bulridge!"

Carla sneered at him. "I'll take my chances." She glanced through the window in the door at where Jason was sitting in the new, unmonitored interview room, his hands placed unthreateningly on the table. "He doesn't look that dangerous."

"The man's a former Army Ranger, a trained killer!"

She just shook her head in disgust. "Fuck off and leave me to talk to my client, Sheriff. And don't you dare attempt to question him again without me present." Without bothering to wait for an acknowledgment, she opened the door and slipped through, closing it behind her with a decisive click.

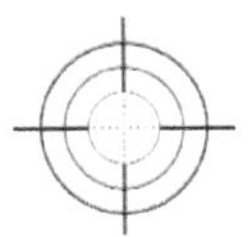

Jason looked up as the lawyer came into the room. She was really tiny, he thought, measuring her by eye against the doorway; maybe an inch or two over five feet, if that.

She was wearing running clothes, jogging shoes and leggings with a windbreaker zipped up over her top, her long black hair pulled up in a ponytail. He wondered if the call from Lulu had interrupted her morning exercise routine.

“Thank you for coming,” he said politely.

A wry smile crossed her face as she stood by the door, measuring him up. “This isn’t a tea party, Mr Hunter.” Her lip curled after she said his surname, as though she’d tasted something bad.

“Please, call me Jason.”

“Carla Ramirez.” She pulled out the chair at the other side of the table, sat down gracefully. Unzipped a pocket of her windbreaker and pulled out her phone. He assumed she would start taking notes as she asked questions, sat patiently to wait for the first.

After a minute or two, Jason found himself frowning. Carla was completely ignoring him. He took the time to study her face, thinking that she was a very pretty woman. She had clear coppery-coloured eyes and a soft golden skin tone that was probably not just a tan, with a last name like Ramirez. There had never been many Latinx folks in Woodvale; he didn't remember any Ramirez family from growing up here. Perhaps she was a recent resident.

A tinny noise drifting to his ears made him blink. "Are you playing a game on your phone?" he asked incredulously.

Carla glanced up at him. "Sure. What else am I supposed to do?"

"Uh… act like my lawyer? I'm assuming you are a lawyer?" McCarthy wouldn't have backed down so easily unless he knew her, surely.

Carla sighed and slapped the phone down on the table. "Mr Hunter…"

"Jason."

"Jason, we both know I'm just here to babysit you until your high-priced big-city lawyer gets here, at which point I can get back to doing my job looking after my actual clients."

The stared at each other, Jason utterly puzzled and Carla contemptuous. Her expression slowly slid towards confusion, though, as he said;

"Ms. Ramirez, I don't know who exactly you think I am, but you're the only lawyer I'm expecting, although I didn't know your name before you walked in here."

"You're Jason Hunter, Philip Hunter's nephew, and your family own this town," she said, but her tone was less antagonistic now, her brow furrowed.

"I think there's been some confusion here, Ms. Ramirez. My uncle might be wealthy, but I'm certainly not. There'll be no high-priced lawyer for me. I'm hoping I can afford your rates."

Carla stared at him for a little while longer, her eyes searching his face as though she could determine his honesty from that alone. "You're serious," she said finally. "There really isn't anyone else coming to represent you?"

"I haven't even been given my one phone call yet."

Carla scoffed. "As if that would matter! McCarthy and your uncle are thick as thieves;

Philip Hunter probably knew about your arrest before it even happened, could have had his legal team on the way here before the cuffs went on!"

"I don't want any part of any lawyers my uncle might bring in. They'd probably be just as crooked as he is."

For the first time, a genuine smile crossed her face, her eyes lighting up, and Jason, startled, realized she was truly stunning when she smiled. "Now you're speaking my language, Mr Hunter."

"Jason."

"Then you'd better call me Carla." She hesitated for a moment before reaching a small, slender hand across the table to shake his. "It's nice to meet you, Jason."

"You too." He released her hand, leaned forward to rest his elbows on the table and said "Now, would you mind telling me what the hell is going on in this town? I know I've been gone a long time, but I really didn't expect Woodvale to have turned into the Twilight Zone while I was away!"

Chapter Four

Carla found herself grinning at Jason's plaintive question. "I was wondering if I'd stumbled into an alternative reality myself, when Lulu called and told me that Philip Hunter's nephew had been arrested for the murder of Julia Bulridge. I figured you had to have been literally caught in the act."

As Jason frowned in apparent confusion and passed a hand over his eyes, she studied him, assessing him anew. He certainly didn't dress like he was rich, she thought; he was wearing a plain black T-shirt and faded blue denim jeans. She'd seen the meager possessions the deputies had taken off him when bringing him in; he'd literally had a set of car keys, a wallet and a cell phone in his pockets.

“Are you cold?” she felt impelled to ask suddenly. The interview room wasn’t much warmer than the temperature outside, and that was barely scraping into the fifties. “Do you have a coat or something I could get for you?”

“I gave my jacket to Julia Bulridge last night. No doubt it’s in an evidence bag by now and will be used to ‘prove’ my guilt,” he said dryly. “It’s fine. I’m pretty hardy, thanks all the same.”

He looked it, she thought, watching the muscles in his arms and chest move under his tight T-shirt as he sat back and laced his fingers behind his head. “The sheriff said you’re an Army Ranger?” she asked.

“Was, yes. I got out about four months ago. I’ve been in Guàlize since then, helping set up an anti-narcotics strike force within their police force, as a civilian adviser. Which is why I’m really puzzled as to how they think they can pin Julia’s disappearance and murder on me, since I can definitively prove that I only got back to the US yesterday morning.”

"I think we'd better start at the beginning," she realized, "and I should really be taking notes. Give me a minute." Going to the door, she opened it and ordered one of the deputies standing outside to get her pen and paper. She knew asking would get her nowhere, but phrasing it as an order made the man jump to attention and hurry away. He returned a couple of minutes later with a fresh yellow legal pad and a pen; she thanked him with a curt nod and shut the door in his face.

"All right," she took a seat and glanced up at Jason again, to see an amused little smile on his face as he watched her. "What?"

"You're tiny and you look about nineteen, but you've got them asking how high when you say jump. You'd have been a great Army officer."

"The military was never in my career plans," but she found herself smiling at the compliment. "And I'm twenty-seven, thank you. Just in case you want to check my credentials, I have a law degree from Stanford and I've been a member of the Idaho State Bar Association for two years now."

“Stanford,” Jason raised his eyebrows, gave her an impressed nod. “What’s a Stanford-educated lawyer doing in Woodvale?”

“I grew up here. This is home.”

“I don’t remember you,” but then, at twenty-seven, she was three years his junior. She smirked slightly as he did the mental math to work it out.

“I remember you, though. Valedictorian, Prom King, captain of the football team, voted Most Likely To Succeed. Graduated top of the class at West Point too, I heard. And yet you left the Rangers as only a First Lieutenant, aged thirty?” She gave him a pointed look.

“I was offered the promotion to Captain but turned it down to leave,” Jason said, apparently unruffled by the remark. “Promotions in the Rangers don’t come easy, either. You’re already the best of the best if you pass Ranger School.”

“Why did you quit?” She should be asking him about the case rather than about himself, but she was honestly curious. There was just something about him; she could easily see him as a leader of men, even the iron-hard commandos of the Rangers.

"Money." He had blue eyes, clear and steady as his gaze locked onto hers. "Aunt Rose's medical bills are pretty hefty. The job in Guàlize pays better than twice what I'd have earned even as a captain."

"You've been paying her medical bills?"

"Sure as fuck ain't my uncle! Pardon my language, ma'am."

Carla waved his apology off, unconcerned. "I had no idea."

"You know my aunt?"

"I do." Carla hesitated. "She's a client of mine."

"Which would mean that you and my uncle don't get on." Jason smiled at her. "I knew there was a reason I liked you. What did you do to piss him off — and why is a smart woman like you still here, where he can make your life damned uncomfortable?"

Carla stared at him. Jason stared back, curious as to whether she would answer. She was the one who dropped her gaze first, picking up the pen and uncapping it.

“I think you’d better fill me in on the timeline of your movements since you arrived yesterday. Hopefully I can get started on establishing an alibi for you.”

As changes of subject went, it was a good one. Jason sighed quietly and nodded, though he still wanted to know the answer to his questions; both how Carla had managed to piss his uncle off and why she was still sticking around.

“My aunt’s neighbor Mrs Barclay called me two days ago,” he began, “to tell me that her condition had worsened.” Something horrible occurred to him then and he started up out of his seat. “Oh, Christ. Does Aunt Rose know I’m here, that I’ve been arrested? If Mrs Bulridge’s body was found in her back yard...”

Carla held out a hand, gesturing for him to calm down. “Jason, I don’t know the answer to your questions, and you can’t go to find out. Do you want to call her?" She pushed her phone across the table towards him.

He grabbed it up but hesitated for a moment before deciding to call the Barclays instead of his aunt. Mr Barclay answered.

"Jason! Good Lord, son, what the heck is going on?"

"I'm being framed," he said simply. "Is Aunt Rose all right?"

"Emma's with her now. She didn't even know you were on your way, we didn't tell her — this has been a bit of a shock, I'm afraid."

Jason pinched the bridge of his nose, screwed his eyes up with distress. "I have a lawyer here with me, Carla Ramirez."

Barclay picked up on the unspoken question. "You can trust her. She's in nobody's pocket."

"That's good to hear," Carla was giving him a cynical look across the table. Jason looked away and concentrated on the phone call. "I didn't do what they're accusing me of, of course, you know that."

"Of course I know that," Barclay said gruffly. "Don't worry about your aunt, Jason. We'll look out for her. Just get yourself out of there as soon as you can."

"Thank you, sir," Jason said sincerely, before ending the call. He slid the phone back across to Carla, who pocketed it.

"Checking up on me?" she said.

"Somebody in this town is trying to frame me for murder. Only prudent of me to make sure you're not in on it, wouldn't you say?"

She nodded at that before picking up her pen again. "Okay, so Mrs Barclay called to tell you that your aunt had taken a turn for the worse. What did you do then?"

"I went to my boss, who immediately granted me indefinite leave to fly home and take care of her. I've known him a long time; he was my captain in the Rangers. He's married to the President-elect of Guàlize's daughter. I promise you there are several hundred people who can place me in Guàlize right up until the day before yesterday, so there's no way I could have been involved in Mrs

Bulridge's disappearance ten days ago... or maybe it's eleven days now."

"How do you know when she disappeared?" Carla was making quick shorthand notes on her pad.

"Saw a poster in the police station, and the Barclays talked to me about her some when I went by their house yesterday evening and asked some questions. Just out of curiosity, because of the odd circumstances."

"Okay. I'll need contact details for your superior in Guàlize..."

He provided the necessary information, and as an afterthought also gave her the phone number for Colonel Brody Cullane, the commander of his former Ranger regiment. Just in case she needed an impeccable character witness.

"I flew to Dallas and picked up a connection to Spokane. Got a hire car there. My airline ticket stubs are in my duffel bag in the motel room."

Carla's pen stilled over the page. "The motel room? You didn't stay at your aunt's?"

“No. Finding Julia on the road and going to report what happened at the police station made it pretty late by the time I got to her house, and all the lights were off. I went to see the Barclays next door instead. They invited me to stay but I decided to go to the motel for the night instead, didn’t want to impose. I ate dinner with them, went to the motel, checked in and went to my room. This morning I woke up, went to the diner and was having breakfast when McCarthy and his Brute Squad turned up.”

“I thought you stayed over at your aunt’s,” Carla spun the pen in her fingers, staring at him thoughtfully. “And I think the sheriff does too, considering the chatter I heard in the bullpen outside. Being at the motel could actually give you a solid alibi. There’s surveillance cameras that cover all the room doors, and there aren’t any rear exits.”

“You’d better get down there and get a copy of the footage before they figure out that I spent the night there and it all mysteriously disappears,” Jason said, half-joking, but when Carla put the cap on her pen and pushed her chair back to get up, he realized that she was taking him seriously. That he wasn't being paranoid.

“It's not paranoia if they really are out to get you, huh?” he said wryly.

“I'm afraid so. I'll get you transferred to a holding cell before I go, but I really need to go confirm your alibi as soon as possible.” She gave him a small smile. “We'll get you out of here, Jason. They jumped the gun arresting you instead of just bringing you in for questioning; I'll get the charges dropped by tonight if I can find that footage.”

“Thank you.” He rose to his feet as she did, realizing how small she really was as he towered over her. He wasn't a giant at five foot ten, but she was really tiny. She looked up at him and smiled a little wider, and he couldn't help but say;

"Please be careful, Carla. I'd really hate for anything to happen to you because of me."

Her expression became serious, and she nodded. "I will. You too. Don't say anything to the police. Just keep your mouth shut until I get back."

"Don't suppose you could get them to give me a coffee? Preferably one without any arsenic in it."

"I'll see what I can do. Right now, you'd better sit down again or they'll probably try and claim that you're trying to be intimidating."

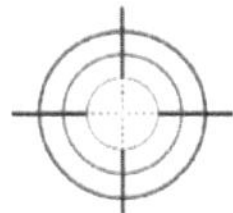

He wasn't all that tall, probably lacked three inches or so on Sheriff McCarthy's height, but the breadth of his shoulders, his military, straight-backed stance, the steady gaze of his blue eyes, all combined to make him a very intimidating man indeed. Somehow, she wasn't in the least afraid of him, though. While there was a certain air of danger about him, an impression of leashed power that could explode into action at any moment, there was also a reassuring calmness that made her feel quite safe in his presence.

Jason raised an eyebrow slowly. "Are you intimidated by me?"

“Not in the least,” she said honestly. “But I have the feeling that whoever’s trying to frame you should be watching their back very, very carefully.”

Smiling, he sat back down, placed his hands on the table. “I’ll plead the Fifth on that, ma’am.”

“Good, because I really don’t want to know about whatever you plan to do. Afterward, though?” she paused with her hand on the door handle, threw him a conspiratorial little smile. “Well, if you need a lawyer, give me a call.”

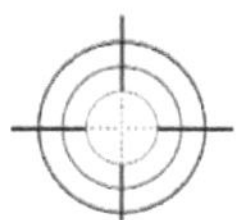

The deputies couldn’t understand why he was chuckling to himself when they came back in to cuff him again and transfer him to a cell. Carla demanded that he be put in a cell by himself.

“You’re claiming he broke a woman’s neck with his bare hands and you want to put him in holding? Come off it. Either he's a danger to anyone around him or he's not."

They didn't seem particularly inclined to argue with her — Jason wouldn't have wanted to either, frankly — and he too suspected that holding would be a bad idea. A man accused of murdering a little old lady would be a target in there, and while he wasn't worried about getting hurt, having to defend himself and possibly hurt other people in the process wouldn't help him any.

"And get him some coffee. None of that nasty shit you guys drink in the bullpen. Go next door to Melissa's and get him a proper coffee."

The deputy held out a hand; Carla gave him a sarcastic eye-roll. "Do I look like I'm carrying my purse? I got interrupted on my jog because you idiots jumped the gun. Get him coffee and I'll fix you up later."

Such was the force of her personality that the man almost jumped to attention. "How would you like your coffee... sir?" he tacked on as Jason gave him a hard stare. Carla snickered behind her hand.

"Black, double shot, two sugars," Jason said. "Thank you, Deputy Allen." He read the man's name tag, gave him an approving nod. An officer to an enlisted man.

Allen took the handcuffs off before they even ushered Jason into the cell, ducking his head and looking apologetic when the cell door closed. Carla waved both men off and Allen hurried away, presumably to get Jason's coffee. Stepping close to the bars, Carla reached out and put her hand on Jason's where it gripped onto the metal, surprising him.

"Hang in there, Jason. I'll be back as soon as I can."

Her fingers were cool and light on his; the impression of her touch lingered long after she was gone and he was left alone with his thoughts.

Chapter Five

Carla couldn't stop thinking about Jason as she left the police station and headed along the street towards the motel. She knew that she should probably go home, shower and change into more professional clothing, but the wry look on his face as he said "It's not paranoia if they really are out to get you" stuck with her, the words resonating in her mind.

It was odd, she reflected as she hurried towards the motel, picking up the pace and starting to jog again, how she had never for a second doubted his assertion of innocence, even before he'd told her his alibi. It wasn't just that she'd encountered the sheriff's corrupt actions before, either; something about Jason himself inspired her trust.

Of course, it probably didn't hurt that he's pretty easy on the eyes, she thought wryly as she turned up the side street that led to the motel. Short dark brown hair, those clear blue eyes, and a deep tan from the hot Guàlizean sun set off a face that wasn't perhaps classically handsome — she was pretty sure his nose had been broken at least once — but definitely held a rugged appeal.

Be professional, Carla, she told herself sternly. He's your client, and he needs you thinking with your brain, not your libido!

The stern self-admonition didn't stop her from thinking that once she'd cleared his name, she might be able to ask him out for coffee, however. Shaking off the errant thought, she entered the motel reception and tapped the bell on the desk.

"Just a moment!" a voice called from the back room, but it was a good couple of minutes before a middle-aged woman came out to stand behind the desk. She looked tired and frazzled, but summoned up a small smile for Carla.

"Well, hello there, Miss Ramirez. What can I do for you?"

"Call me Carla, for a start." Carla put on her friendliest expression and smiled. "It's Nora, isn't it?"

The woman nodded, returning the smile. "That's right. What can I help you with then, Carla?"

"Your security footage from last night. You had a guest who's been accused of a crime, but he claims he was here all night. I want to take a look."

"Sure," Nora shrugged amiably. She obviously hadn't heard about Julia's body being found yet, Carla thought. Nora opened the small side door behind the desk and beckoned her inside. "Come on through and I'll run it back for you. What time did he arrive, do you know?"

"You had a lot of guests last night?" Carla asked curiously.

"Well, it is hunting season. Think we've got about five who are staying at the moment for that? And one guy who arrived last night, a Mr Hunter… that your man?"

"It is," she admitted.

"He was nice, a real gentleman." Nora nodded. "What'd he do?"

"I can't discuss that, Nora. Client confidentiality, you understand… and I'm pretty sure he didn't do it anyway."

"Sure." Nora shrugged, not remotely bothered by the evasion of her question. She sat down in front of a computer and lifted a stack of papers off a second chair so Carla could sit down. "He got here 'bout nine, I think." She reached for the mouse. "Let's take a look."

Nora was off by less than ten minutes. The timestamp showed 8:51 PM when Jason's solid figure first entered the view of the cameras, walking into the motel's forecourt with his duffel bag over his shoulder.

"There he is," Carla murmured, watching his image grow larger as he approached the camera. He went out of view a few seconds later and Nora flipped the view to the camera inside the reception office.

The two women watched the footage in silence as Jason spoke to Nora, filled in a sheet of paperwork and handed over his credit card to be swiped before being given a room key in return.

“I gave him Room 31,” Nora said, blushed slightly as she added, “It’s just been refurbished, got a brand new bed and everything, it’s the nicest room we have. I’m supposed to charge more for it, but he was so nice that I… didn’t.”

Carla hid a little smile. “He said he slept very comfortably here,” she fibbed, making Nora smile more widely, her blush deepen a little further.

“Well. He only paid for the one night, but I do hope he comes back.” She clicked the mouse again. “And lucky for you, one of the cameras points almost right at the door of Room 31.”

“So it does,” Carla murmured, watching as they saw Jason approach the door, let himself into the room and close the door behind him. The light went on, and they clearly saw him standing in front of the window beside the door, looking around for a few moments. He sat down on the bed in full view of the camera, took his boots off and pulled his shirt off over his head.

It wasn't the clearest image in the world, but both women got a good look at the thick, honed muscularity of his chest and shoulders.

"Oh my goodness," Nora said, her flush spreading to encompass her whole face. "Do you think he's going to...?"

Carla certainly hoped so, but Jason stood up at that moment and crossed to the window to pull the curtain closed.

"Oh," Nora said in distinctly disappointed tones, and Carla let out a giggle.

"Now, now, I know that was a lovely view but we really shouldn't want to be Peeping Toms."

Nora laughed too, a bit shamefaced. "You're right, of course." She took her hands away from her blushing cheeks, reached for the mouse again. "Well, if he says he stayed in his room all night, I guess we can fast-forward..."

She put the footage on ten-times speed and they watched in silence as the light behind the curtain clicked off. There was no movement whatsoever in the frame until the image began to lighten with the dawn. The curtain was pulled back not long after; Nora immediately slowed the replay down to real-time speed and the two women caught a view of Jason's muscled back this time as he walked away from the window towards the bed, opened his duffel to get out a clean T-shirt and pulled it on. He left the room a few minutes later, walking out of the frame to the right, away from the office. Nora selected the forecourt camera again, and the last sight they had of Jason was him walking away from the motel in the direction of the diner.

"That seems pretty conclusive," Carla said.

"There's no way out of those rooms except for the door and the front window," Nora nodded. "Do you need a copy of these?"

"Yes, please. Everything from say, eight last night until eight this morning?" That would more than cover the time Jason had spent at the motel.

Nora opened a drawer in the desk and fished out a USB key, plugging it into the computer. "It'll take a few minutes to copy over. Want a coffee?"

"That sounds wonderful," Carla admitted. "Unless I'm keeping you from your work?"

Nora shook her head. "I'm on reception duty this morning and we haven't got any guests booked in. Mr Hunter was due to check out, though, what should I do about that? He didn't take his duffel bag with him when he left."

Carla dearly wanted to collect the bag, but if she did, the police could claim she'd tampered with evidence. "I expect the police will come and get his things soon, Nora, don't worry. If they don't, I'll pay for another night at least. I'll leave you my credit card number and you can charge it if you need to, so you don't get into trouble."

"Well that's mighty kind of you," Nora said happily, getting up to switch the coffee machine on a nearby table on after she'd started the file transfer. "Thank you very much."

Ripping a blank sheet from the yellow legal pad she was still carrying, Carla wrote the details down, folded the sheet and handed it over to Nora. "Only if you need it, mind, and no shopping sprees," she said with a smile. She barely knew Nora, but the woman had been more than helpful. They'd shared a certain camaraderie while watching Jason move around shirtless on camera, a little secret between them of how much they'd enjoyed it.

They were sipping their coffee, Nora chattering away telling Carla about how her eldest son was graduating high school that year and hoping to study pre-law at the University of Idaho, when a voice snapped;

"What's going on here? I'm not paying you to sit around drinking coffee!"

Nora seemed to shrink back inside herself. "Sorry, Mr Wells," she set her cup down and stood up. "We didn't have any customers yet today. Just Carla — Miss Ramirez — come in to..."

"And that's another thing, nobody's allowed back here," Wells snarled. Carla knew he was the motel owner, a mean-spirited man who pinched his pennies until they squeaked. He'd be hell to work for. She suddenly felt very sorry for Nora, who was dumping her coffee down the sink and washing the cup.

"You need to leave," Wells turned his scowl onto Carla.

"As you wish." She moved over to Nora, set the cup down so the other woman could wash it up. "Don't tell him why I was here," she breathed softly into Nora's ear. "Make out we're friends and that I just came by to catch up." Wells was clattering around in a filing cabinet on the other side of the room; Carla was pretty sure he couldn't overhear. Nora gave an infinitesimal nod.

Turning around, Carla stepped in front of the computer, hand sneaking behind her back to pull the USB drive from the slot and slip it into the pocket of her windbreaker. "Thanks for the coffee, Nora," she said loudly. "Let's catch up at Melissa's next time, though. And I'll have a look and see if I can find those old pre-law textbooks for Nate. He can read up over the summer, get a head start!"

"That'd be great, love," Nora said in a grateful tone. Carla glanced back at her and got a conspiratorial wink; confident that Nora wouldn't let on why she'd been there, Carla departed. She was halfway down the street when a police cruiser passed her, the sheriff at the wheel; she turned to watch it pull into the motel forecourt.

The sheriff talked to the Barclays, she realized; found out that Jason had elected to get a motel room for the night. Urgency filled her suddenly and she quickened her pace to a fast run, wanting to get to her office and upload the surveillance footage on the key to secure storage as soon as possible.

Carla's office was in the front room of her home. Letting herself in, she headed straight to her desk and plugged in the USB drive. She'd seen the transfer complete on the screen behind Nora while they were talking, knew that the files were all there. Wondering if she was being a bit too paranoid, still she took the time to password-protect the files and upload them to every online storage site she used. After a couple of minutes' thought, she sent an email to a friend from law school who was now with the FBI, with a note.

'If you don't hear from me within 48 hours, please open these files. They provide the alibi for a man named Jason Hunter who I think is being framed for murder...'

Satisfied that she'd done all she could to back up the data, she sent the email, took the USB stick out of her computer and considered where to hide it. Finally, she shrugged. If the worst happened, she'd wind up telling whoever questioned her exactly where it was anyway; Carla had no illusions about her ability to withstand pain or coercion. She tossed the stick into the top drawer of her desk.

Finally, it was time to head for the shower and make herself look a bit more professional. She needed to go see Rose Hunter and the Barclays; she was pretty sure Jason's first question next time she saw him would be about his aunt's well-being.

On her way back out of the house wearing a smart pantsuit and clutching her briefcase, something occurred to her. She backtracked to her office to make a phone call to the senior county DA, a man from another town she was on quite good terms with. She'd worked summers as a paralegal in his office while attending law school. What she learned had her shaking her head with disgust; the sheriff hadn't even bothered to consult the DA's office before calling the judge for the arrest warrant. Marcus Devereaux, the DA, made furious noises down the phone when she filled him in.

"Copy those files to me," he requested. "If they show what you say they do, I'll have the warrant rescinded immediately and your man will be free to go. I've spoken to the ME this morning and he's provisionally given the time of death as around midnight."

Carla closed her eyes and let out a sigh of relief, at having Jason's innocence completely confirmed. "I'm sending them through to you now," she said, "I'm sorry if I seem a bit paranoid, but after that DNA evidence cockup in the Moritz case..."

"I completely understand, Carla," Marcus told her. "We both know McCarthy's crooked. We just have to catch him at it and he's gone, I promise you."

She thanked him again before hanging up and going to get her car. First stop, Rose Hunter, to check on her health before going back to Jason and giving him the good news.

Chapter Six

The street where Rose Hunter lived was a quiet cul-de-sac, which was a good thing this morning, Carla figured. The sheriff's department had the entire street blocked off with crime scene tape, though there was nobody there actually manning the barrier. Shrugging, Carla stepped over the sagging tape and headed for Rose Hunter's house, only to find, to her horror, the old lady on the phone with the bank attempting to arrange a loan against her house so that she could raise bail money for Jason while Mrs Barclay looked on helplessly.

"I tried to stop her but she's stubborn as a mule," Mrs Barclay told Carla.

“I’ve got it,” Carla told her, removed the handset from Rose’s hand and turned the phone off. “You’re not mortgaging your house. Jason would rather stay in jail than see you do that, but it’s not necessary anyway. I’ve established his alibi and the DA is going to have the arrest warrant rescinded. He’ll be free by tonight.”

Rose had been about to start a furious tirade, but only the words “How dare…” had slipped out by the time she registered what Carla was saying. Tears started in her faded blue eyes.

“Bless you,” Rose choked out, fumbling for Carla’s hand. “Bless you.”

“It’s all right, Mrs Hunter.” Carla gently pressed on the fragile fingers, horrified by how much more frail Rose had become in the few weeks since she’d last seen her. Paper-white skin drawn tight over her high, elegant cheekbones made her look almost skeletal. She wore a silk scarf wrapped around her head to hide her lack of hair and there was an IV cannula permanently emplaced in the back of her left hand.

She's dying, Carla realized, and soon. "I'll have Jason with you within a few hours," she promised fervently. "My word on it."

A single tear slipped free, traced down Rose's cheek. "Bless you," she whispered again. "I didn't ask for him to come back. I was afraid something might happen, though I never thought they'd go this far..." She closed her eyes against more tears. "It's not his fault. None of it is his fault."

Carla hesitated, and then decided that she had to ask, even though it was really none of her business. "What was not his fault, Mrs Hunter? I don't understand why this has happened."

Rose sighed and opened her eyes again. "You'd better sit down, dear. Emma, would you make us some tea?"

"Of course," Mrs Barclay bustled importantly off to the kitchen while Carla took a seat.

"Jason's grandfather Peter and my husband Paul Hunter were identical twins," Rose began. "Their father was a very successful man; he owned the sawmill and built half the town. He left his estate equally to his two sons and expected them to run it together. It was only a few months later that Peter and his wife were killed in a car accident; Jason's father David survived. He was only eleven. Paul and I of course were his guardians, and David was raised with our son Philip." Rose sighed mistily, looking out of the window. "David was a lovely boy; I loved him like my own. Philip was five years younger and I thought it would be nice for the two to be brothers."

"Why am I having the sinking feeling that it didn't work out like that?" Carla asked, as Emma Barclay returned with the tea things and began to pour.

"Philip hated David from the first moment he came to live with us, even though David was of course just devastated from the loss of his parents. Philip insisted we were spoiling David, that we didn't want him, Philip, any more now we had David, which was ridiculous, of course - Philip was our son! He was jealous of everything David had, everything he did. When David started dating Jessica Bateman — prettiest girl in town, she was — Philip did everything he could to try and sabotage them, silly childish pranks but so upsetting. In the end David decided to leave town and join the Army, and Jessica went right along with him. They got married and had Jason. They were very happy even with the Army posting David away a lot of the time."

Carla sipped her tea in silence, listening as the old woman reminisced. Rose Hunter had truly loved her orphaned nephew and his wife, she thought, and her own son's behavior had obviously distressed her immensely.

"David was killed in action in '95," Rose went on, "and Jessica didn't know what to do. Jason was just a little boy; she had nowhere to go but back here, back to her family."

"I'm assuming, then, that Jason is still the heir to half the family businesses?" Carla said, a little puzzled. "Because he told me that 'my uncle is rich, but I'm not'."

Rose let out a little moan at that, her hand shaking. "Oh God, I wish he was, Carla. I wish he was. It's all my fault..."

"Please don't distress yourself," Carla reached out to her instinctively.

"Paul, my husband," Rose collected herself and carried on, "he'd always treated David like his son just as much as Philip, despite Philip's jealousy, and David trusted him to look after his share of the business. I was co-executor of David's trust, and I believed Paul was doing the right things, of course — I had no reason to think otherwise. So when he asked me to sign papers which transferred different holdings around, of course, I did it. In the end it turned out that Paul had been transferring failing assets into David's name, out of his own, and it all snowballed — not long after David died, his estate was bankrupt."

"It wasn't your fault," Carla reassured her quietly, reeling from the bombshell that his own uncle had deliberately destroyed David Hunter's fortune, and by extension, Jason's.

"I should have known. Should have checked up," Rose shook her head. "I will never forget the look on Jessica's face the day Paul told her. He was smug about it, didn't even bother with the fake sympathy. Told her right out what he'd done. I thought she was going to hit him."

“I think she was very restrained if she didn’t hit him,” Carla said wryly.

“She couldn’t really, with Jason standing right there clinging to her leg. She just turned on her heel and walked out. I was so shocked; I hadn’t realized up until that moment what had happened. I confronted Paul and asked him why he’d done it; he claimed it was all for Philip.” Rose shook her head. “Well, I didn’t say anything, but the next day I took my car and I drove all the way to Spokane and sold every single bit of my jewelry. I emptied my bank account and spoke to a divorce lawyer. Then I drove back to Woodvale and gave all the money to Jessica.”

“I bet that went down really, really badly with your husband,” Carla said after a moment of shocked silence.

Rose’s smile was tight. “The Batemans invited me to stay with them. Jessica’s father was the sheriff back then; a fine man. I owe him my life, because I’m quite sure Paul intended to kill me when he came looking for me that night with a gun. He was screaming and ranting like a madman, shouting that he would kill Jessica and Jason too. I was never so frightened in my life." Shaking her head, Rose said quietly "Joe Bateman shot him dead in the street."

"Wow," Carla's mouth hung open. She'd heard the story before; it was the biggest scandal that had ever happened in Woodvale, but to hear it from Rose Hunter herself put a new perspective on things. She'd never realized Rose had walked out on her husband because Paul Hunter had deliberately ruined his nephew's estate.

"Philip was in his last year at college. He came home and took over all the businesses, never bothered to graduate. Paul died before he could change his will, so I did get at least the small amount he'd left me — enough to buy this house, at any rate." Rose waved her hand around vaguely. "I invited Jessica to bring her son and come live with me. She was like the daughter I never had."

All this explained why Jason was so fond of the old lady, Carla realized. She was more like a doting grandmother to him than a great-aunt who wasn't even related to him by blood.

“What happened to Jessica?” she had to ask.

“Oh, well, when Joe Bateman retired he and his wife bought a condo in Florida, and they used to go spend the whole winter down there before they eventually moved there permanently. Jason was already gone to West Point by then, and Jessica used to go down to visit her folks quite often. She fell for a man down there and remarried. They own a little business down there, a pool maintenance company; doing all right for themselves.” Rose shrugged, a little sadly. “I’m happy for her, but I do miss her. She writes to me every week at least. So does Jason, come to that.”

“Why didn’t you move away too?” Carla had to ask, though she suspected she knew the answer; it was the same one she herself had given Jason at the jail.

“This is my home,” Rose said, and Carla nodded, unsurprised. “I was born here in Woodvale and all of my happiest memories are here. Despite the bad things that have happened too, I wouldn’t ever have wanted to live anywhere else.”

Carla knew exactly how she felt. She smiled at Rose and took a sip of her tea as the old lady sat back in her chair and sighed wearily.

“You'll really get my boy out of there today, Carla?” Rose asked after a minute.

“I will. I'm just waiting for a call back from the DA to let me know that the arrest warrant has been rescinded.” Carla took her cell phone out of her bag, glanced at it. As though the very act had caused it, the phone started to ring. “Excuse me.”

Carla went out onto the house's front porch to take the call, leaning on the porch railing. “Carla Ramirez,” she said in greeting.

“It's Marcus Devereaux at the DA's office. I'd ask what the hell is going on in that town, but I already know.”

She sighed and pinched the bridge of her nose. “Tell me.”

“I called McCarthy to ream him out for not coming to me to discuss the possibility of prosecuting this as a murder case before he took out an arrest warrant for Jason Hunter. He was smug as hell; claimed the case is cut and dried. Julia Bulridge's body found in old Mrs Hunter's back yard, wearing Jason Hunter's jacket, neck broken by someone with great strength."

From where she was standing, Carla could see the yellow police tape still fencing off the back yard. There were two officers from the crime scene unit still there combing the place carefully, two more standing guard at the side gate, warning curious passers-by away. Not that there should be any passers-by, since Rose Hunter's house was at the end of the cul-de-sac. Carla shook her head and returned her attention to the call.

"That doesn't mean he killed her; and since he has a rock-solid alibi of only having got into the country last night, it explains absolutely nothing about where she's been for the last couple of weeks."

"I led in with that, I assure you," Marcus said firmly. "And then he tried to tell me that Jason Hunter having stayed at the motel last night couldn't be proved since the surveillance cameras are on the blink and the night clerk doesn't remember him."

Stunned, Carla took a moment to process that. "Wait... you're saying that the camera footage is already deleted and Nora intimidated into silence? It was literally minutes after I left there, that McCarthy turned up at the motel! I saw him drive in!"

"When I told him you'd already emailed me a copy of the footage, he changed his tune real quick. Said the motel owner must have made a mistake," Marcus' tone was dust-dry.

"Yeah, right," Carla said with equal cynicism.

"I'm on my way over to Judge Robards' office now. I'll meet you at the police station within the hour and we'll get your man freed."

"Thanks, Marcus," she said gratefully.

"You're welcome, hon," there was a laugh in his voice. "Come over to dinner soon. Suze keeps telling me to invite you, there's some guy she works with she wants to introduce you to."

"Yes to the dinner, no to the matchmaking," Carla said with a chuckle. Hanging up, she headed back inside to give Rose the good news.

“I should have him here with you in no more than a couple of hours,” she promised. “I’ll call if there’s a delay for any reason, okay?”

“I’ll be fine, dear.” Rose patted her hand. “Emma’s here to keep me company and two other friends are coming around shortly for a game of bridge.”

“I think that’s them now, actually,” Mrs Barclay peered past the lace curtain at a car just pulling up outside. “Yes, it is. You go, Carla. We’ll keep Rose busy until you and Jason get back.”

Chapter Seven

Carla arrived at the police station just before Marcus; the tall, snappily-dressed DA held the door open for her as she walked up to him with a smile.

“Got it?” she nodded at the folder of papers in his hand.

“Yeah. Judge Robards wasn’t keen, but when I flatly informed him that I would refuse to prosecute due to evidence-tampering already having occurred, and also advised him about you sending a copy to your buddy at the FBI, he caved pretty quickly.”

Carla shook her head, lips tightening. “Another one of Philip Hunter’s cronies,” she said softly, making sure to keep her voice too low for anyone other than Marcus to hear.

"Sometimes I think you and I are the only folks in the legal system in the entire county who aren't dirty."

Marcus's answering smile was fake, designed to fool onlookers that they were having a friendly conversation rather than the very serious one which was actually taking place. "I've put feelers out to people at the State Supreme Court, Carla, but I've got to move carefully. Hunter's an important man, he knows a lot of people. If I ask the wrong question to the wrong person…" for a moment, the lines at the corners of his eyes looked very deep. "I've got a wife and two kids, Carla."

"I know," she answered quietly, "and I promise you I would never do anything to risk Suze and the kids. Never."

"I know." He took a deep breath and squared his shoulders. "Come on, then. Let's get the black sheep of the Hunter family out of jail."

"I think you've mixed your metaphors," Carla said wryly. "I'm pretty sure that Jason Hunter is actually the guy you'd want at your back. He's just the only one who was smart enough to get the hell out of Dodge and make a life for himself somewhere else."

"Clearly smarter than all of us, then," Marcus said with a small grin, "for all our fancy Ivy League degrees."

Carla smiled, unable to argue with that, and turned the smile on the desk sergeant as he looked up at them warily.

"Get Sheriff McCarthy," Marcus said, his tone cold and flat, "now."

Footsteps outside his cell brought Jason out of a light doze; while he wasn't tired, life in the Rangers had conditioned him to take sleep whenever and wherever he could find it. He didn't bother to get up, not yet, just rolled his head to the side to see whoever came to his cell door. The deputies had put him in a cell at the far end of the row, with no neighbors, nobody to talk to. Not that he was particularly interested in chatting with whoever else might be locked up in Woodvale's lockup.

It was Deputy Allen, with Carla and a tall, good-looking man in his forties with weary lines around his eyes, wearing a nice suit and well-polished shoes. Carla was smiling, a tight, triumphant little smile. Deputy Allen looked nervous and the tall man just looked tired.

"This is Assistant District Attorney Devereaux, Jason," Carla said. "Get the door open, Deputy Allen."

"Yes, ma'am," Allen said, fumbling with a large ring of keys.

"I have here an official rescindment of your arrest warrant, Mr Hunter," Devereaux held up an official-looking sheet of paper. "You are free to go."

"That was fast," Jason said, impressed, rolling easily to his feet as Allen finally got the door open. "You're good, Ms. Martinez. Didn't need those high-priced city lawyers after all."

She laughed, smiling up at him as he came to the door and offered his hand to Devereaux to shake. “I already apologized for that.”

“You did, and were forgiven, but that doesn’t mean I won’t keep mentioning it,” Jason grinned back at her. “Seriously, though, thank you. Do I take it that I’m no longer under investigation?”

“The tapes Carla sent through are good enough for me,” Devereaux replied. “I would decline to prosecute any case brought to me predicated on what I’ve already seen, including the clear evidence-tampering by the sheriff’s department. Which will be investigated, I assure you.”

Deputy Allen’s neck turned red, but he didn’t say anything, just stared resolutely ahead as he led the little group back down the corridor.

“Your wallet, sir,” Allen said as they reached the sergeant’s window at the front; a shallow plastic tray was proffered. The contents of his pockets, which had been confiscated and itemized when he was brought it. It wasn’t much; just his wallet and cell phone.

“I had a motel room key, as well,” Jason said as he pocketed his things.

“It’s been returned to the motel.”

“Right.” He figured that his rental car and the rest of his belongings had probably been impounded as evidence, but frankly at that moment they weren’t his concern. He’d worry about them all later. After he’d seen Aunt Rose.

“Would you like a ride to your aunt’s house?” Carla asked, and he silently blessed her for reading his mind.

“Yes, please.”

“My car is right outside.” She said a quick farewell to Deveraux and then led Jason out to the car park, pointing to a silver Toyota Camry. “That one’s mine.”

Nodding, Jason slipped into the passenger seat and sat still while Carla started the car.

"I saw Rose," Carla said, needing to fill the tense silence. "She's okay."

"No, she's not okay. I know how sick she is. I've been talking to her doctors," Jason said tersely.

"Fine, then, she's not okay. She's dying. But your getting arrested didn't make her any worse than she already was. She's looking forward to seeing you." Glancing sideways at him as they pulled out onto the street, Carla added "Put your seatbelt on. The sheriff's gunning for you. You better not so much as jaywalk while you're in Woodvale, Mr Hunter, or you'll find yourself behind bars again, and next time you might not actually have an alibi I can use to get you out."

A half smile touched Jason's lips as he fastened his belt. "Thank you for the advice. And I thought we were on a first name basis, or did I do something to piss you off?"

"No." Carla smiled too, her eyes on the road. "Just... stay innocent, huh, or we'll have to go back to being lawyer and client again."

"Oh, I'm most definitely not innocent." There was a dirty innuendo to the words that her body reacted to even while her brain told her she shouldn't.

"Behave, or I'll tell your aunt you can't keep it in your pants."

"Hey, she helped raise me through my horrible hormonal teenage years. Aunt Rose knows very well how I'd react to a woman as gorgeous as you."

Carla found herself laughing, charmed by Jason's outrageous flirting. Flipping her indicator on, she checked her mirrors and made the turn into the cul-de-sac before pulling up outside Rose Hunter's house.

"Well, here we are." She wasn't sure what else to say.

"Thanks for the ride. And for the — well, everything else." Jason didn't seem in any hurry to get out of the car. "Send me your bill, huh? I'll be here with Rose until — well, until."

Carla nodded, her expression sympathetic. "I'll see you around, Jason."

He nodded and shot her a smile before seeming to steel himself to get out of the car. Carla watched him walk up the driveway and step up onto the porch of the house, pausing briefly before opening the door without bothering to knock. It wasn't until the door had closed behind him again that she put the car back into Drive and moved off, heading home, her mind on the man she'd just left behind.

"Jason, darling!" Rose Hunter cried out as he entered through the front door, the door she'd never bothered to lock except at night. She'd lived here almost as long as Jason had been alive, and all of her neighbors had been here as long or longer.

"Don't you dare get out of that chair." He crossed the room in a few massive strides, stooped down to put his arms around her, horrified by how frail she'd become since his last visit not quite a year ago.

Thin arms locked around his neck, but there was no strength in her grip.

"You shouldn't have come," she whispered against his cheek, "but I'm so glad to see you."

He didn't want to let her go, stayed bent over and holding on until she laughed breathily and pushed at him.

"Get off, you great lump. Let me look at you."

Forcing a smile to his lips, Jason let go and straightened up, taking a step back and spreading his arms wide, turning around slowly. "Do I meet with your approval?"

"You look wonderful. Tanned, but much more relaxed than the last time I saw you this tanned."

"Well, Guàlize is a lot nicer than Syria," he joked. "Far smaller chance of getting shot at, too. Great food, good hours, fantastic pay. Couldn't be happier. You should come visit."

"Well, the photos you've been sending me look wonderful." She gestured towards the tablet lying on the table beside her chair. "Maybe I'll come, when I feel better."

They both knew she wasn't going to feel better. Treatment had kept the cancers slow-growing, but she'd never had any kind of remission and the time was now fast-approaching when her body would shut down completely.

Jason knew what her answer would be, but he had to make the suggestion anyway. “We could go tomorrow. Seriously, my boss is married to the President-elect’s daughter. One phone call and I could have the President’s private plane waiting for us at Spokane in the morning… Ariana’s a doctor, too, she’d see to your treatments…”

Rose was shaking her head, smiling gently. “It sounds lovely, dear, but this is my home.”

Her softly voiced words silenced him at once, and he sighed, sitting down beside her and taking her fragile hand in his. “All right. Then I guess we’re both here for the duration. I’ve got as much leave as I need -- and I’m not leaving you.”

For several minutes, neither of them spoke, and then Rose tried to squeeze Jason’s fingers, in reality just exerting a gentle pressure.

“I’m glad you’re here.”

He wanted to cling on and never let her go, but instead he took a deep breath and forced a smile. “Wild horses couldn’t keep me away, Aunt Rose. Now. What jobs have you got saved up for me to deal with?”

“Well.” She smiled, laugh lines creasing deeply at the corners of her eyes. “I might have a few little things to deal with. I don’t like to ask Bill Barclay to do too much, he’s not as young as he used to be.”

Jason returned her smile. “Point me to the toolbox, then. Let’s get this place smartened back up.”

It wasn’t until a couple of hours later, as he carefully smoothed spackle over a dent in the plasterboard by the front door, that he realized Aunt Rose was having him smarten the house up to maximize its value, so he would get a good price for it once she was gone.

Briefly, he leaned his brow against the wall and took a few deep breaths.

What am I gonna do when you’re gone, Aunt Rose?

She'd never stopped sending her little care packages of homemade cookies, always accompanied by a chatty, handwritten letter, even in the last few months as the cancer took hold. He had to wonder if the first he'd have known of her death was when the hospital called him, as her named next of kin.

The thought just about tore his heart in two.

Chapter Eight

The following morning, Carla was sitting at her desk lost in thought, tapping her pen slowly against the edge of her keyboard, when a movement outside the window caught her attention. Not that many people walked past her window; she was on a main road and like everywhere else in America, most people drove. Especially when it was raining.

The figure walking along the sidewalk was distinctly recognizable. Jason Hunter was marching past her window, heading downtown it looked like, still only wearing a T-shirt and jeans even in the miserable weather.

"What the heck," she muttered to herself, jumping to her feet and hurrying to her front door, grabbing her umbrella from its usual spot hanging from the coat rack. Popping it up as she headed outside, she called "Jason!" loudly after him.

She had to call twice more, running along the street after him, before he heard her over the rain and turned around.

"Carla?" Rain slicked his tanned skin, soaked his shirt to those magnificent shoulders. Carla suddenly understood what made men so interested in wet T-shirt contests for girls. Jason's pectoral and abdominal muscles were perfectly outlined by the wet, clinging fabric. She stared, unable to drag her eyes away, missing Jason's next words.

"Sorry, what?"

"What are you doing here? You're not exactly dressed for the weather." He gestured at her coatless state.

"I could say the same for you! I saw you walk past my window in the rain. Why don't you have a coat? Come in to my place, you're soaked through!"

With a shrug, Jason followed her as she turned and headed back up the street without waiting for an answer. She was wearing different pants to the ones she'd had on yesterday, a lighter gray, the rain dark-spotting the hems above the high heels of her black boots.

"Do you always wear heels?" he asked without really thinking about it, as he followed her up the steps into her law office.

"If you were five foot nothing tall, you'd always wear heels too," Carla glanced back over her shoulder at him as she folded up her umbrella, grinned. "Did you see Jurassic World? I can run like that in heels. Damn well would if a T-Rex was chasing me, too." She walked past the door into her office and opened another door at the rear of the hallway, leading him into a brightly lit kitchen. "Here." Opening a drawer, she grabbed a small towel and threw it at him. "Not that it will do much good."

Jason smiled back at her, mopped the water from his face and head. "Not much, no. And I don't think the T-Rex would dare chase you. She'd recognize an alpha when she saw one."

Carla wanted to laugh, he could tell, the corners of her eyes crinkling up adorably. "I'm not sure if I should be complimented or insulted."

"Well, I meant it as a compliment." Jason smiled at her. "Strong women do it for me."

He honestly hadn't expected her to blush, but she did, the skin over her cheekbones noticeably darkening before she turned away and switched on the coffee machine.

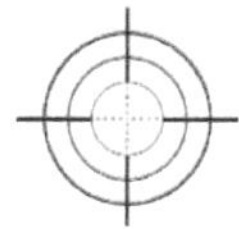

"How's your aunt today?" Carla asked, changing the topic after a brief silence.

"Doing okay. The nurse came by this morning and another friend stopped by to visit with Aunt Rose. House really isn't big enough for that many people."

“So you decided to go for a stroll in the pouring rain?” She glanced cynically at him, getting cups down from a cupboard.

“I was going to buy some more clothes, actually. Since I think my duffel got sent off to a forensics lab God only knows where, and my jacket is definitely evidence anyway. I’m sure I’ll never get that back even if my duffel does turn up.”

“Why is your jacket evidence?” Carla frowned as the coffee machine started to sputter.

“I’m pretty sure that Julia Bulridge’s body was found wearing it. She stole it out of the back of my car when she took off again.”

“That’s right, you did tell me.” She turned to look at him, noting the way he’d propped a hip against the kitchen counter and was standing with his arms folded, casually at ease. The pose certainly did good things for those thickly muscled arms, she thought, before reluctantly tearing her gaze away and focusing on his face. The corners of his mouth quirked up, blue eyes glinting at her.

Dammit, he knows very well I’m ogling him.

“So you’ve got nothing but the clothes you stand up in, literally?”

“That’s right. I didn’t bring a lot, just a couple of clean shirts and another pair of pants, but one set of clothes is a bit minimalist even for me. Plus, though I’m not gonna keel over in a bit of cold and wet, a jacket would be really nice.”

“So you were walking into town to buy some clothes.” She nodded, turning away again to pour coffee. She pushed the sugar bowl towards Jason, watched as he added a couple of spoonfuls to his cup.

“Well, Aunt Rose doesn’t have a car any more, and my hire car is also God knows where. I was planning to stop in at the police station and ask about that, much though I don’t particularly want to.” He grimaced at the thought.

“You shouldn’t do that on your own,” Carla said immediately. “I’ll come with you.”

“Are you even still my lawyer? And come to think of it, you need to give me a bill for your services so far, please.”

“Do you have any money?”

“Well, the things I did get back from the police included my wallet and my phone, so yeah.” He grinned. “If you mean in my bank account, yes to that, as well. My job pays pretty well.”

A little abashed at having asked so bluntly, Carla nodded. “Okay, I’ll type you up an invoice and drop it by. It’s not that much, I haven’t done much...”

“I beg to differ. Your quick work at the motel made sure that the surveillance footage couldn’t be hidden away. Without that to prove my alibi, I’d still be in a cell.”

Conceding that was probably true, Carla nodded slowly. Jason set his cup down then, moved past her to the sink.

“D’you mind?”

She wasn’t sure what he meant, so she just nodded, and then gaped as he peeled his wet, clinging T-shirt off and wrung it out over the sink. Her brain just froze up completely, leaving her drop-jawed and pop-eyed as he turned back to her.

"Do you have some sort of rule about not getting involved with clients?" Jason asked softly.

"Uhn?"

"Because I'd really, really like to ask you on a date."

Tearing her eyes off his chest with enormous difficulty, Carla dragged her gaze up to his face. "I was thinking the same thing," she admitted, "that once this was finished, I'd like to ask you out for coffee."

He grimaced slightly, pulled his wet T-shirt back on, struggling a little as the fabric clung at his skin. "I don't think it will be over as quickly as all that. Philip Hunter doesn't want me in Woodvale. This was just a golden opportunity to get rid of me; he won't stop here."

"I think I'll take my chances," Carla decided.

"I was hopin' you'd say that." He took a step closer to her, and Carla felt her body react, her pupils dilating, her pulse accelerating, her breath coming shallow.

"So, after I've bought some more clothes and we've paid a visit to the police station, could I maybe buy you a coffee? Because I gotta tell you, your coffee absolutely sucks." His eyes crinkled at the corners.

She spluttered indignantly. "It does not!"

"It's terrible, and you know it." He grinned at her. "What have you done to those poor beans?"

Carla realized then that she hadn't tasted it, frowned at her cup. Took a sip. "Oh my God. Oh my God, I forgot to change the filter!"

Jason broke up laughing. "I thought maybe you were trying to poison me there for a minute!"

She hung her head, but saw the funny side and started to laugh too. Dumping what was left of her coffee in the sink, Carla told him;

"You're on for the coffee date, but I'm buying. Since I just tried to poison you."

Carla drove Jason to Woodvale's tiny mall first, to get some fresh clothes. He didn't pick out much, just a couple pairs of pants, a few T-shirts, a fleece jacket and a windbreaker, all in plain, dull colors. He was trying to blend in, Carla realized as she watched him pay for the items, charming the store clerk with his smile. Freshly dressed in new, dry clothes, he came to stand by her.

“Anything you need to get, while we’re here?” he gestured around the mall.

“I’m good, thanks,” she shook her head. “Let’s go drop by the police station and see if we can at least get your wheels back.”

“My passport’s in my duffel, as well. I could care less about the rest of it, but that would be a hassle to replace.”

“When are you heading back?” she asked as they walked back to where she’d left her car. He hadn’t mentioned a departure date.

“I’m not going anywhere while Aunt Rose needs me.” Jason’s face closed down, and Carla realized that he intended to stay until his aunt’s suffering was over, however long that might be. Not long, she suspected, considering Rose’s fragility.

“I see,” she said quietly. “There’s no pressing need for you to be back in Guàlize?”

"I've got compassionate leave for as long as necessary." Jason's smile was tight. "My boss knows Aunt Rose well. Or, he knows her care packages. The homemade cookies she always sent me were a huge hit in the regiment, especially when we were on deployment."

That made Carla chuckle softly, thinking of the burly, hard-bitten soldiers of the Rangers calling down blessings on Jason's Aunt Rose as they eagerly devoured her cookies.

There was a new man on the front desk at the police station, one Jason hadn't seen before. He was younger, round-faced, and smiled eagerly at Carla as she stepped up to the desk.

"Hey, Floyd," Carla's demeanor didn't soften as she planted both hands on the desk and stared at him. "Now. We can do this the easy way, or we can do it the hard way. My client Mr Hunter here has been cleared of suspicion in Mrs Bulridge's murder case, and he wants his things back."

"Things?" Floyd asked, drooping a little at Carla's severe expression and all-business tone.

"Yes. His duffel bag and its contents, which were taken from his room at the motel when McCarthy searched it. Since my client has been cleared, his belongings are not evidence, the police have no cause to withhold them from him, and I want them returned. Right now."

Floyd stuttered briefly before saying "I'll be right back, Miss Ramirez," and getting up from his seat.

Carla and Jason were both surprised when Floyd returned only a couple of minutes later, carrying two transparent plastic bags. The duffel was in one of them, its contents in the other; Floyd laid an itemized list down on the counter.

"If you wouldn't mind checking off your belongings and signing for them, sir?" he said very politely to Jason.

"Make sure everything is there," Carla said, and Jason picked up the list, glanced it over.

"That's everything I brought with me, yeah." Ripping open the plastic bags, he repacked his duffel. "Looks like everything's there." He flicked through the pages of his passport, checking that his long-term Guàlizean visa was still in place. "Yep, everything's fine."

Floyd held out a pen and Jason took it. "Wait," he paused in the act of putting pen to paper. "My hire car. The keys aren't here."

"No, the car's at the impound lot. They have the keys there. You'll have to go down there to get it back." Floyd cringed as Carla shot him a death glare. "I can call ahead. Make sure they know to release it to you."

"You do that." Carla turned on her heel. "We're going for coffee, and then we'll be going to pick up the car, and they'd better have authorization to release it."

"Yes, Miss Ramirez," Floyd said miserably to her retreating back.

Chapter Nine

"Why is that poor man so scared of you he just about shit his shorts when you scowled at him?" Jason asked as they left the police station.

"Floyd?" Carla smirked to herself as she put her umbrella back up, led him across the parking lot and to the building next door, which turned out to be a large bakery and coffee shop. "We were in the same year at high school. I know stuff about him that he would really rather nobody else found out about. Especially considering his chosen career path."

Jason snickered. "Ah, the good old blackmail technique."

"It's not blackmail," Carla said primly, though her smirk remained. "I've never actually threatened him with revealing his secrets."

"Because you didn't have to. His own overactive imagination has already conjured up every nightmare scenario that could occur if you did." Jason shook his head. "You're a terrifying woman, Carla Ramirez." Leaning down towards her ear as she reached to open the door, he whispered "I find that really sexy."

She was quite glad that she had her back to him and he couldn't see the sudden flush of color that heated her cheeks.

"Jason!" a woman's voice squealed then, and a pretty blonde darted out from behind the counter and flung herself on him. "Jason Hunter, you are a sight for sore eyes!"

"Melissa," laughing, he hugged her tightly, kissed her cheek. "I can most definitely say the same thing for you!"

She smiled at him when he set her down; reached up to frame his face in her hands. "Well, look at you. The years have been very kind. More handsome than ever!"

"And you've grown up from a beautiful girl into a stunning woman," Jason said in response, taking her hands and squeezing them. "What are you doing here; you work here?"

"I own the place," Melissa said with simple pride, beaming from ear to ear.

"You do?" Jason looked around admiringly, noting the pretty, unaffected decor, the delicious coffee-and-sugar scents, the fabulous array of cakes and savories in the shining glass cabinet counters. "Well, haven't you done well for yourself!"

"Well, me and the bank," laughing, she looked around. "But yes, I built this business all on my own."

"Nobody gets coffee anywhere else in town," Carla put in, feeling oddly left out. And jealous, even though she knew Melissa was happily married. Once upon a time, Melissa Darling and Jason Hunter had been the golden couple of Woodvale High; the football star and the head cheerleader, prom royalty, the people everyone aspired to be.

"You certainly don't," Melissa smiled widely at her, letting go of one of Jason's hands and reaching to touch Carla's arm affectionately. "Your usual, honey?"

"Please. What'll you have, Jason?"

He looked up at the board of gourmet coffees listed, grinned. "Double shot of Guàlize Gold, black with two sugars, please. And something tooth-rottingly sweet from the cake cabinet."

Melissa chuckled at that. "I know just the thing. Grab a table, I'll bring it all over." She let go of Jason's hand with one last squeeze.

"She's married now, you know," Carla found herself saying as she took a seat.

"I do, actually. She and Tim sent me an invite to their wedding. I was in Afghanistan at the time, didn't get the invite until a month after the wedding actually happened."

"Oh," Carla felt oddly deflated. "They have two kids. Twin girls."

"That, I didn't know," Jason said. "How old?"

"Uh... about four, I think? Not old enough to be in school yet. Melissa's mom has them during the day; I often see them in the park when I drive past. They both look just like Melissa, blonde and beautiful."

"That she is," Jason smiled across the room in fond reminiscence as Melissa bustled around behind the counter, smiling and instructing her staff. She'd been his first crush, his first girlfriend, his first kiss — they'd even taken each other's virginity one sultry summer night long ago.

"Maybe you should have stayed here and married her instead of joining the army," Carla said half-sulkily, kicking herself mentally for feeling jealous — but then she'd spent almost the entirety of her high school years feeling envious of Melissa Darling. Why stop now?

"Good God, no," Jason said so vehemently that she was actually surprised. "She wanted to stay here and settle down and do the white picket fence thing. I couldn't get out of Woodvale fast enough."

That brought a little half-smile to Carla's lips. "Me too," she admitted, "but I still wound up back here somehow. It's like the Twilight Zone; keeps sucking you back in somehow."

"You must have had better memories here than I did."

"Oh come on, Jason, you were Mr Perfect back then! The football coach still talks about you as the one student he had who could have gone pro, your name is still on a bunch of trophies and plaques on the wall. Every student who came after you was measured up against your perfection."

Jason cocked his head, studying her curiously. "Including you?"

Carla thought about denying it, eventually shrugged ungraciously. "I was valedictorian my graduating year," she admitted finally. "With a GPA of 4.2 and the highest SAT scores anyone from Woodvale has ever achieved. Went on to graduate Stanford summa cum laude - and my name's all but forgotten at Woodvale High."

"Because you're female and you weren't a football star," Jason surmised, shaking his head in disgust. "Sexism is still very much alive and well, tragically." Reaching across the table, he put his hand over Carla's. "You impress me, Carla. Very much. No matter what anyone might think, I know your value. I'd still be rotting in a jail cell if it weren't for you, for starters. You are not less than anyone, and most certainly not me. I'm just a soldier — a mercenary these days, technically."

"I don't think a contract to train elite Guàlizean troops is quite the same thing as your run-of-the-mill mercenary," Carla had to smile at that.

"And when my contract is over, what then? Unemployed, homeless, and possessing only a moderate skill at kicking ass. Whereas you, you're smart, Carla. You got the education, the law degree. Folks will always need attorneys, in Woodvale more than anywhere."

"Maybe that's the real reason I came back," Carla said softly. "Because I knew I was needed here."

"There's no better reason." He was still holding onto her hand, gazing deep into her eyes. She lost herself gazing back. His eyes were so blue, depthless. His thumb traced a slow, warm circle on the back of her hand.

A small, embarrassed cough made them both startle and look up. Melissa stood there, a tray balanced on one hand.

"I'm so sorry to interrupt, I didn't realize..." she cut her eyes at their joined hands.

Carla went to pull her hand back, embarrassed, but Jason tightened his fingers over it. "I asked Carla on a coffee date," he told Melissa.

Melissa beamed at both of them. "Good for you," she said approvingly. Carefully, she set down two steaming mugs, put a plate at Jason's elbow, and retreated.

"That looks wicked," Carla said, glancing at the plate and laughing. A gigantic slice of Melissa's famous triple chocolate and honeycomb cheesecake with mounds of ice cream and whipped cream on the side looked deliciously tempting.

"I see that she took me seriously about the tooth-rottingly sweet." Jason laughed, let go of Carla's hand reluctantly and picked up the fork resting on the edge of the plate. "Looks fantastic."

"I'll be able to hear your arteries hardening from here," she chuckled, picking up her coffee mug and inhaling the aromatic steam rising from it as she sat back to watch him eat. He forked off a large chunk and ate it, eyes widening.

"Mm. Mm!"

"Good?" Carla was fairly sure she knew the answer, as those blue eyes half-lidded with pleasure and he forked off another piece eagerly.

"Mmmm." It was a low, happy rumble. She was startled when he held the fork out towards her, licking crumbs of flaked chocolate off his lips. "You should try some."

"Oh, no. I really shouldn't," she tried to demur, but it did look really, really good. She'd never order a whole slice for herself, but maybe just a bite... leaning forward, she parted her lips.

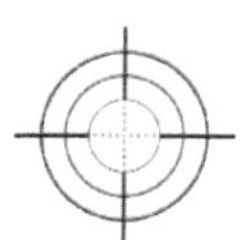

Jason's own lips parted as he gazed at Carla; slowly he lifted the fork to her lips, watched as she sucked the cheesecake off the tines, her lashes fluttering down to lay softly on her cheeks as she savored the sweet treat.

"Mm," she agreed a few moments later, eyes still closed. "Delicious."

Jason actually had to adjust himself in his seat as his pants became painfully constricting. Carla looked impossibly sensual like that, and his already strong attraction to her spiked even further. It took a couple of minutes for him to realize that he was just staring at her, his mouth open, the cake fork clutched in his hand still suspended in midair.

"Aren't you going to eat any more?" Carla reached out, took the fork and stole another bite of cheesecake.

She knew very well what she was doing to him, Jason suddenly realized, as her eyes laughed at him. "You really are trouble," he said, and she chuckled aloud.

"Maybe."

"I'll get you back," he threatened.

"Will you now?" She laid the fork back down on his plate and picked up her cup. "How are you gonna do that, then?"

"Get wet in the rain and peel off my shirt in your kitchen again?" Jason grinned, getting a little of his composure back.

"Yeah, that works. I guess we could probably call it evens, considering that you already did that." Carla's eyes dropped to his broad shoulders, lower down his chest. "Do you have a particular fondness for T-shirts a size too small?"

They were both snickering when a sudden silence fell in the room. Jason's head snapped up, and he cursed himself for not paying closer attention as he caught sight of the men who'd just entered.

Sheriff McCarthy moved up to the counter with a confident swagger to his step, completely ignoring Jason, but the man behind him stopped and stared, first at Jason, then at Carla.

Jason's jaw clenched as, for the first time in five years, he came face to face with his uncle, the man who'd helped deprive him of his rightful share of the Hunter businesses.

Philip Hunter.

"Jason," Carla said very softly. "Do you want to leave?"

"I think we'd better." He fished in his pocket for his wallet, but saw Melissa shake her head at him across the room.

"I've got a tab. Let's just go," Carla said quietly, and they got to their feet, abandoning their coffee and the half-eaten cake.

Nobody in the room said a word as they left, apart from the sheriff who was loudly ordering his coffee. Philip just stared at Jason as they moved towards him. Jason didn't drop his gaze, and though Carla tugged at his sleeve, trying to caution him away, he came to a stop in front of his uncle and stared him down.

They could have been brothers, Carla thought; Philip Hunter was in his early fifties but certainly didn't look it. Though his hair was cut in a more civilian, manicured style than Jason's military clip, they had the same intense blue eyes, the same shape of face, the same stubborn set to the jaw.

That stubborn set told Carla that they weren't going to get out of this without words, at the very least, being exchanged. Even McCarthy had finished ordering his coffee and turned to stare. His hand twitched towards the gun at his hip, and Carla very deliberately moved, putting herself between McCarthy and Jason. He'd have to shoot through her first, and there were an awful lot of witnesses in here. Unless, of course, he just shot over her head, she thought wryly.

"Jason," Philip acknowledged finally. There was no sound in the bakery, not even the coffee machine. From the corner of her eye, Carla saw Melissa wringing her hands behind the counter, the look on her face one of fear.

"Philip," Jason said into the tense, singing silence, his voice flat and hard.

"Do you plan to be in town long?"

"As long as I need to be."

It was Philip who dropped his eyes first. "How is my mother?" he asked then.

"None of your fucking business."

An audible gasp went around the room at that, and McCarthy's hand tightened on his gun grip, but Jason went on, uncaring.

"You were perfectly happy to let her lose her home in order to pay her medical bills. I'm willing to bet the bank manager called you right after Rose first called him. She was just about to sign the papers on the loan when I found out about it and stepped in, though. So don't pretend that you give a flying fuck about her well-being."

There wasn't really a lot Philip could say to that. Rose's medical bills would have been pocket change to him. He tried, though.

"She didn't ask me for help."

Jason's expression was pure scorn. "She didn't ask me for help either. Funny how that goes, ain't it?"

"She's still my mother, Jason!"

"You abdicated that right when you tried to deny her even the little she was left in Paul's will," Jason snapped back. "And then you spent years making damn sure that my mother couldn't even get a job in this town. Well fuck you. I'm not gonna dance to your tune, not now, not ever. Rose doesn't want to see you, so stay the fuck away."

Philip said nothing, and Jason finally turned on his heel and headed for the door. With a last glance at McCarthy, Carla followed, caught up with Jason in the parking lot standing with both hands on the hood of her car, breathing deeply. The rain had stopped and there was just a thin, damp fog in the air. It suited her mood, Carla thought, feeling dreary and depressed, the date which had started — and continued — so promisingly, now utterly ruined. She glanced back at the bakery. They wouldn't be visible from inside, not where they were standing right now. Going up to Jason, she put one hand on his, feeling the cold metal of the car's hood against her fingertips.

"I wanted to hit him," Jason said, his voice ragged.

"I know. McCarthy was looking for an excuse, though."

"Yeah." He didn't say anything else, just turned his hand under hers to grip her fingers, looked down at her, his eyes blazing with barely-suppressed emotion.

"Come back to my place," Carla said, and they both knew exactly what she was asking.

"I'm in no mood to be gentle."

"Rough will suit me just fine." One corner of her mouth quirked up, and Jason nodded, his gaze boring into hers.

"Let's go."

Chapter Ten

Neither of them spoke a word on the short drive back to Carla's house. Unlocking the front door, Carla stepped inside and immediately found herself pushed up against the wall by Jason's hard body as he kicked the door shut behind them. She was too short for him to kiss easily so he hitched his hands under her thighs and lifted her, encouraging her silently to wrap her legs around his waist as his mouth sought hers for a heated, ferocious kiss.

Carla was more than willing; she was eager. Her arms wrapped around Jason's neck, her legs around his lean hips. She pressed her fingers against the back of his head, nails scratching against his scalp, pulling him closer as she kissed him back with equal ferocity.

Jason shrugged out of his fleece jacket, suddenly far too hot as Carla twined herself around him. “Bedroom,” he took his mouth from hers long enough to say.

“Upstairs,” she panted back. “Too far...”

He couldn’t agree more, but up against the wall in the hallway wasn’t really going to work either, and the floor was tiled, not carpet. “I want a bed,” he pulled back from her eager, seeking mouth. “For what I want to do to you... we need a bed.”

Carla moaned with need, pressing wet, sucking kisses against his neck. Sharp little teeth met in his earlobe as she urged him to hurry, almost making Jason lose his mind entirely. He growled under his breath as he strode towards the kitchen, remembering having seen the stairs at the back of the room. He took them two at a time, Carla’s slight weight nothing to a man who’d spent days at a time carrying a pack and weapons load heavier than she was. Although, he thought vaguely, he hadn’t usually had to do so with his pants constricting brutally on an erection straining to escape.

Carla's bedroom was simply furnished, he saw, taking in with a quick glance the plain cream walls, the scrubbed-pine timber furniture, the neutral bedspread. The one bright spot in the room was a lovely wall hanging in shades of ocher and rust; he thought it might be a Cree piece, dimly thought that he would ask Carla about it later. She was tugging demandingly at his shirt, though, grinding against him with her hips rolling in slow circles, and Jason forgot everything else in his frantic need to get inside her.

They fell to the bed together, scrabbling at each other's clothes in a desperate rush, needing to feel skin on skin. Carla ripped Jason's new T-shirt; he accidentally popped the button off her pants. His bootlace knotted and he cursed fiercely.

"Please," Carla almost sobbed it, fighting out of the last of her own clothes as Jason yanked at the offending bootlace. He finally managed to free it and hurled his boot across the room before turning back to gaze at her hungrily.

She lay back against her pillows and opened her arms to him in welcome.

Carla's skin was golden all over, a soft dusky flawless amber. Midnight curls between her thighs did nothing to hide the evidence of her desire as she deliberately lifted a knee, giving him a perfect view of her pussy, wet and shining with slick.

"Oh, fuck," Jason rasped, staring. "Fuck, you're so beautiful."

She was glorious, her slight form firmly muscled, small breasts tipped with plump, pouting brown nipples he was suddenly desperate to taste.

"I could say the same for you," Carla was gazing back at him ravenously, taking in his powerful torso, the hard-earned, thick biceps muscles bulging as he rolled onto the bed and reached for her.

"I've wanted you since I first laid eyes on you, sassing McCarthy and his brute squad," Jason confessed, hands closing almost reverently on her breasts. "All that fire and passion. All I could think about was what you'd be like in bed." His fingers tightened on her nipples, squeezing just to the edge of pain, and Carla bucked up against him with a throaty moan. "What you'd taste like." He looked down at her pussy, and in answer she bent one slender leg and hooked it up over his shoulder, pressing on his back with her heel.

"Why don't you find out?" she suggested.

Jason needed no further invitation to slide down the bed, pressing open-mouthed, hot kisses against her stomach as he went, nestling himself in between her thighs, strong hands moving back under her thighs so both legs were over his shoulders.

The first lick was a long, slow stripe from her opening all the way up to her clit; Carla moaned and shuddered as the second followed the same path before Jason started teasing over her clit with his tongue, lapping rapidly.

He certainly knew his way around down there, Carla thought hazily as Jason's tongue swirled and dipped. A thick finger joined in, delicately parting her labia, swiping slow circles around her entrance before suddenly plunging deep.

"Oh fuck, yes," she panted, hips jolting upwards unconsciously; Jason chuckled deeply against her before closing his lips and starting to suckle on her clit, each draw of his mouth perfectly in sync with a thrust of his finger. Soon he added a second finger, and then a third, making Carla yelp, feeling stuffed full as he sped up his thrusts, crooking his fingers so that their callused pads rubbed right over her most sensitive spot with every firm stroke. Her own fingers clenched in the sheets, wordless cries spilling from her lips as a sudden explosion of fireworks behind her eyes sent her spiraling off the edge.

Jason grinned as Carla's silken internal muscles sudden clenched spasmodically on his fingers. She wasn't quiet in her passion, ecstatic cries ringing from the walls as her small body bucked on the mattress, her heels digging into his back as she held his mouth against her, right where she needed it. He kept lapping, slower and gentler as she came down from the orgasmic high, teasing the tip of his tongue in a circle around the swollen, pulsing bud of her clit until she took a leg off his shoulder and pushed at him with one small foot.

“Enough,” she mumbled.

“Yeah?” he considered carrying on anyway. He still had three fingers thrust deep inside her, crooked them for another tentative stroke at her G-spot. She groaned.

“Jason. Too sensitive!”

“All right,” he sighed, withdrawing his fingers gently and moving back. She opened heavy-lidded eyes to peer at him as he sat back on his heels; gave him a languorous smile.

“Just gimme a minute,” Carla slurred. Her whole body was buzzing from the afterglow of that spectacular orgasm; the intensity only prolonged by Jason’s expert mouth and fingers.

“One minute and one only,” Jason said, “and then I’m nailing you to this bed.”

The mere thought, coupled with the promise in his words, made Carla shudder with a little shock of renewed lust. She looked down his body to where one hand was curled around his cock, jacking it slowly. It looked just as thick and powerful as the rest of his honed muscles, a pearly bead of pre-cum glistening at the tip. She licked her lips unconsciously, staring.

"Yeah," Jason said hoarsely, "you got a damn pretty mouth. Been thinking about seeing those soft lips wrapped around my cock, too. You want that, huh?"

She did; she wanted to taste him, feel the heavy weight of him in her mouth. Licking her lips again, Carla nodded. "Come fuck my mouth," she demanded, making him grin. He moved up over her, kneeling astride her shoulders, leaning forward to put his hands on the headboard so that the swollen, flushed head of his erection hovered a scant inch above her lips. She darted her tongue out to lick off the droplet of pre-cum, making Jason groan.

"Turnabout is fair play," Carla said primly, eyes laughing up at him, before that wicked little tongue darted out again, this time to worry lightly at the frenulum.

"Jesus," Jason choked out as her hands came up and joined the play, one wrapping as far as she could around the base of his cock while the other curved around his thigh from behind to lightly cup and roll his swollen, aching balls between her fingers. "Oh, fuck, Carla!"

She tugged firmly on his cock, pulling him down lower, encouraging him to spread his knees a little wider. Trusting that she knew her own limits and wouldn't choke herself, Jason gave in to the silent demand and shifted lower, letting her take his cock deep into her open mouth. He flung his head back in ecstasy, gazing towards the ceiling, savoring the wet, delicious heat of Carla's mouth, the dexterity of her tongue as it worked and swirled over sensitive spots he'd barely remembered he possessed. She was sucking on him like he was a favorite lollipop and she was desperate to get all the flavor.

"No," Jason rasped suddenly, pulling back sharply and making Carla cry out with loss as his cock jerked out of her mouth. "No, gorgeous though your mouth is, I don't want to come there. Not this time." His blue eyes were dark as he looked down at her lying there, lips wet and puffy, her eyes glazed with passion. “You got condoms, Carla?”

“Top drawer,” she waved vaguely to her left, and he reached over to the nightstand, scrabbled around for a minute, pushing aside silky underwear until his fingers closed on a square box. He stayed kneeling above her face as he rolled the condom on, before moving back to kneel between her thighs.

“Still not feeling gentle,” Jason said a little gruffly, “so you might want to grab onto somethin’.”

She took him at his word, reaching out to grab onto the timber slats of the wooden bed frame behind her head, wrapping her fingers firmly around the thicker center one and bracing herself.

“Good. Told you I didn’t want gentle.”

Jason looked down at Carla, lying there eager and welcoming, and couldn’t hold back any longer. Kneeling between her thighs, he wrapped his hands around her hips and lifted, bringing her ass up to position her perfectly as he leaned forward, his sheathed cock straining to push inside her. She bent her knees and planted her feet on the mattress, gasping with pleasure as the tip of his cock glanced over her clit before pushing slowly into her sopping entrance.

“Oh, yes,” Carla breathed, throwing her head back against the pillow. “Oh hell yes.”

Jason had no words; it felt too good, pressing deep inside Carla and feeling her tight tunnel slowly expand to accommodate him. She was a small woman and he was generously endowed; he took it slowly, carefully. At least until she hooked a leg around his hip and tugged demandingly.

“More. Come on, Jason, I need more, give it to me!”

There was no way that he could resist that half-demanding, half-pleading note in her voice, the look in her eyes as she gazed up at him. One rough thrust of his hips and he was fully seated, inside her all the way to the root of his cock, groaning with pleasure as tight slick muscles squeezed down on him hard.

"Fuck, that feels good," he muttered. "So damn tight."

It was Carla's turn to be unable to speak; beyond words, her head tossed from side to side on the pillow, her hips rolling as Jason's deep penetration pressed on all the right spots deep inside her. Low, wordless cries spilled from her lips as his fingers tightened, holding her still, before he began to move in slow, shallow thrusts, at least at first. Reassured by her very obvious pleasure at what he was doing, he soon began to speed up, ramming hard and fast, long deep strokes that drew ragged screams of pleasure from her.

Feeling the tingling sensation at the base of his spine that warned his own climax was fast approaching, Jason took one hand off Carla's hip and put it between them to thumb at her clit, rubbing quick circles over it even as he kept on slamming into her. Her cries increased in pitch, her hair thrashed from side to side on the pillow, and suddenly she was there; clenching down on Jason so hard he briefly saw stars, her small body twisting and writhing under his.

He had no chance of holding back against the tight, wet grasp of her pussy sucking on his cock, even if he'd wanted to. With a low, guttural moan he let go, slamming out a few more shuddering thrusts before throwing his head back and roaring his ecstasy to the roof as blast after blast of hot cum jetted from his cock deep inside Carla's hot tunnel.

Coming down from the throes of her own climax, Carla still found enough presence of mind to appreciate the view as Jason's arm and chest muscles tightened, the cords in his neck standing out as he flung his head back. He looked magnificent, primal; it was an incredibly intense moment as she felt the heat of his seed flooding deep inside her, his cock throbbing slowly as it pulsed. She moaned with a little shock of renewed pleasure as he twitched inside her, and he looked down at her and smiled, his blue eyes heavy-lidded with satisfaction.

Slowly and carefully, Jason lowered Carla's hips to the mattress, slipping out of her at the same time. Knowing he should go to the bathroom and clean up, right at that moment he didn't feel up to anything but laying down beside Carla, every muscle relaxed, his whole body humming with pleasure as she curled up to his side and laid her head on his chest. He wrapped one thickly muscled arm around her and stroked the small of her back gently. She made a contented little sound, and Jason smiled.

“You okay there, beautiful?”

“Mm-hm,” she agreed, nuzzling her cheek against his chest. “Yup.”

“First time I've seen you not runnin' your mouth,” he teased, and she lifted her head to shoot him a warning glare. He snickered, rolled towards her a little way to kiss her again.

The kiss had none of the urgency of their first, but was no less passionate. The initial heat of their mutual need spent, they had the time to explore each other's needs and likes, to taste and tease. Carla scrambled up to sit astride Jason, never breaking the kiss, her hands eagerly exploring the thick planes of his chest and shoulders. His hands came up to play with her breasts, thumbing over her nipples until she moaned into his mouth.

"You better get off me," he broke the kiss to say hoarsely, "because I need to change this condom."

She made a face, but saw the sense in his argument. "Hurry up," she ordered, her tone brooking no argument as she climbed off to let him up, "because when you come back I'm gonna ride you like a buckin' bronc."

"Oh Jesus, thank you for bringing this woman into my life," Jason said fervently with a glance up at the ceiling as he scrambled off the bed and made hastily for the bathroom. By the time he returned, Carla already had another condom open and ready; he needed no urging to lie back and let her roll it on for him. Already hard again, he groaned with pleasure as her fingers wrapped around him, tracing his shape, cupping his balls and squeezing experimentally, discovering what he liked.

"Come and hop up," he invited, wrapping a hand around the base of his cock, making it stand straight up. "I want to see those pretty breasts bouncing in my face as you ride me.

Want to see you taking your pleasure on my cock."

Carla smiled as she mounted up, swinging a leg across his thighs and positioning herself over the tip of his cock. She had to stretch; he wasn't a small man by any means. Sweat broke out on her brow as she lowered herself slowly onto him.

"That's it," Jason had to clench his fists in the sheets to keep from grabbing Carla's hips and just ramming up into her, she felt so good; but if he did that he'd hurt her. She was small, and she needed to take him at her own pace. "Oh fuck, yeah, sweetheart, that's it. Yep. Yep, take it all ahhhh." He trailed off in a low moan as she pushed down suddenly, adding a little twist of her hips.

"Mm, that's good," Carla hummed in her throat, leaning forward to kiss Jason, her hardened nipples rubbing on his chest. He grunted as she shifted before his hands came up to claim her hips, grasping firmly and holding her still when she would have pulled back a little.

"Nope, right there."

"Guh," was all she could say. The angle meant that the head of his cock was pushing right against her G-spot, and he knew it, from the smirk he was giving her.

"Feel good?"

"Ugh!" Deliberately, she dug her nails into his shoulders. "Let me move, dammit!"

He laughed roughly before letting her sit up, his hands moving to her breasts, tugging and tweaking at her nipples. "Come on, girl. Said you were gonna ride me. Show me how well you can gallop."

Carla laughed breathlessly, her hips beginning to rock back and forth as she braced her hands on her thighs to steady herself and began to flex her leg muscles, setting up a quick pace. "Sure you can take it, soldier?"

"Try me."

She was more than willing to give it her best shot; she sped up the roll of her hips, enjoying the way Jason's roughened fingertips worked her nipples, sending bolts of pleasure racing through her. He let go suddenly and she let out a cry of outraged loss.

“Here,” Jason grabbed her hands, lifted them. “You take over. I want to play with your clit again.”

Carla had no problem with that, grasping her nipples to rub and squeeze, knowing even better than Jason exactly how much pressure to use. He groaned at the sight.

“Fuck, that’s so sexy! What you do to me...” he shook his head, and then his warm palm was pressing against her mound, thumb and forefinger delving down into her cleft and pinching lightly at her already-sensitive clit.

“Oh god I’m gonna come again,” Carla gasped, feeling the familiar tingle beginning to thread along her nerves.

“Me too, beautiful,” Jason’s voice was hoarse, his hips bucking up roughly, taking over as she broke, unable to continue the rhythm. “Oh fuck, you’re so beautiful when you come...” she was clenching down on his again, her lips parted on a long low moan as her head tipped back, her hands stilling on her breasts. He let go of her breasts and clamped his hands on her hips, holding her steady as he thrust faster and harder, chasing his own release. It didn't take long to find it, the pulse of orgasm racing through his body. He stilled, pressed as deep inside Carla's willing body as he could get, savoring the feeling of her walls clasping his pulsing cock.

Chapter Eleven

"Tell me about Julia Bulridge," Jason requested. They were lying together in Carla's bed, her head resting on his chest, his hand lightly stroking her hair. "Her case seems really personal to you. Was she a client of yours?"

"No, she wasn't," Carla said with a sigh, shifting over and propping her chin up on her hands, meeting his eyes. "I didn't know her, not to speak to, though once the posters started going up I realized I'd seen her around town. You know how it is."

Jason nodded. Woodvale was a small town; you might not know everyone in it by name, but live here long enough and you'd eventually know most folks by sight. Carla and Julia had probably crossed paths multiple times without speaking, in the grocery store or Melissa's bakery or at the library.

"Were you involved in the search for her?" He guessed that the whole town had been mobilized to search, at least in the woods close to town.

Carla nodded. "Yes, I went out on several of the search parties. I had to." She squeezed her eyes shut for a moment, seeming to steel herself. "This wasn't my first rodeo, you see. Four years ago, my mother went missing."

Jason's arms tightened around her instinctively as he stiffened with shock. "Your mother?"

"She had early-onset dementia." Carla was obviously struggling to get the words out, she to whom words seemed to come so naturally, so Jason stayed quiet, waiting patiently for her to find the ones she needed. "I was working in Seattle, studying for the Washington State bar exam. When Mom got sick I came back home to look after her, but it progressed so fast. Within a couple of months she didn't know me, didn't know anyone. She grew up in San Antonio, Texas, had started talking about going back there, and I was looking into taking a trip, maybe even getting her into a care home down there if it would make her feel more comfortable to be in a place she found familiar."

Tears welled in Carla's eyes as she spoke, the memories obviously extremely painful for her to dredge up. Silently, Jason stroked her hair, trying to offer comfort as best he could.

"Mom usually took a nap in the afternoon. I'd taken to going for a short walk or nipping out to get groceries while she slept; the day she disappeared I wasn't even gone more than half an hour but when I got back, the front door was open and she was gone."

"Were you living here back then?"

Carla shook her head almost violently. "No, we lived on Stony Creek Road."

Jason's lips pursed in a silent whistle. He knew Stony Creek Road well. It led nowhere in particular, just off into the woods before finally petering out. Mainly used by logging trucks, there were a few small houses scattered off the road on five or ten-acre lots, folks who kept a few animals for the most part.

"You'd gone into town?"

"To the grocery store, just to pick up a few things. Mom was so self-sufficient, she kept chickens and a milk goat, grew most of her own vegetables, even baked her own bread. She still liked to do all that stuff, and I helped her with it. Her doctor said it would help with the dementia, to try and keep her reminded of her usual routine. We'd run out of coffee, though, so I thought I'd just take a quick drive to town to get some; it's only a ten-minute drive each way and she always slept for at least an hour."

"Did you lock the door?" Even as he asked, Jason knew it was a stupid question. Folks who lived down Stony Creek Road didn't bother locking their doors because most of them had nothing worth stealing. It was very possible that the front door hadn't even had a working lock, and if it had, Carla's mother could certainly have opened it from the inside.

“No,” Carla said, her eyes downcast. “I just pulled it closed behind me, I never even thought. It wouldn’t have kept Mom in anyway if she decided to wander.”

“But a forced lock would have been evidence that she didn’t leave of her own accord,” Jason said.

“Which is why I’ll never stop kicking myself for not locking it, because then the police might have taken me seriously. It was twenty-four hours before the sheriff finally accepted that Mom was a missing person and deigned to help with the search. Until then, I was on my own.”

“I’m so sorry,” Jason said, knowing the sentiment was inadequate but feeling the need to express it anyway. “You never found any trace?”

“Nothing. Not a damn thing, and that’s why I just can’t buy it. We lived on the land, but Mom didn’t like the woods. She’d never have wandered off there, and if she’d walked on the road somebody would have seen her, picked her up. Everyone who lived down that road knew her, and there’s no way she could have walked far enough for me to miss seeing her on my way back, either." Carla's voice rose in pitch as her distress increased. "I've never been able to accept that Mom just disappeared, and Julia's disappearance brought it all back to the surface, because the circumstances were just so similar, you know? And then you turn up with this crazy story about Julia out in the woods and she turns up dead and I… I totally believe you, which means what happened to her? And did whatever happened to her happen to Mom?"

She was shaking with emotion, tears running down her cheeks. Wrapping his arms around her and hugging her tight, Jason said firmly "Whatever happened to both Julia and your Mom, it's time to make sure it never happens to anyone else."

"Wh-what do you mean?" Her voice was muffled against his neck, but easily discernible.

"It means, it's time to unearth whatever dirty little secrets Woodvale has been hiding. The sheriff's department clearly aren't taking the disappearances seriously, so I will."

“Jason, what are you planning to do?” Carla pulled back, lifting her face to look at him.

“I’m gonna help you investigate.”

“This isn’t your fight... and you already have quite a target on your back,” she shook her head, frowning with concern.

“It became my fight the moment Julia Bulridge begged me to help her,” Jason disagreed. “I failed her, and I feel like part of the blame for her death can be laid at my feet. If I’d managed to keep her with me and got her back into town, or if I’d stayed out there in the woods and found her myself instead of going to the sheriff’s office, would she still be alive? Because I have to wonder if she wasn’t killed solely because I saw her. They had to produce her one way or another, and dead with the murder pinned on me was the only convenient way to do it. The only way it could be done so that she couldn’t tell anyone about where she’d been.”

Carla stared at him, wide-eyed. “You think somebody was holding her somewhere? Why?”

“That’s the sixty-four thousand dollar question, isn’t it?”

They were both silent for a minute, considering, before Carla said quietly “And the other important question is who, isn’t it?”

“If we can answer the who, we can figure out the why. Or figuring out the why might lead us to who. Either way, too many folks have gone missing without trace in this town. That ends now.” His jaw was set, his expression determined. He reminded Carla of an attack dog on a leash, solidly muscled and terrifyingly powerful, patiently waiting for his owner’s command to unleash fury.

Jason Hunter would be a formidable adversary, but he was the kind of ally Carla had never had in her quest to figure out what had happened to her mother. With him at her side, she felt a surge of something that almost felt like hope.

"Will you promise me," she said, "that you won't quit on me?"

"Rangers don't quit, ma'am." He met her eyes steadily. "While my first consideration right now has to be for Aunt Rose, I promise you that I won't leave Woodvale until I help you solve this mess."

"Good enough for me," Carla said with a nod, and leaned forward to seal the deal with a kiss. Jason's muscled arms tightened around her and he flipped them suddenly, rolling her to her back.

"Somebody's gotta watch your back," he said seriously. "You've had mine, so far. I want you to know that I've got yours, Carla, whether this works out or not." He nodded down at their naked bodies, pressed firmly together. "No matter what happens, I'll never leave you in the lurch with the bad guys closing in."

That deserved another kiss, so she wound her arms around his neck to deliver it. Feeling him harden against her thigh again, she pulled back and smiled at him. "Do you have anywhere you need to be?"

"Not right now," he shook his head, smiling back at her. "You?"

"No appointments until tomorrow morning."

"Well, I'd better get back to Aunt Rose's in time for dinner, but until then, I'm all yours."

"Excellent." Reaching out to the nightstand, she felt in the open drawer for the box of condoms. "Let's not waste any time, then."

Grinning, Jason took the packet from Carla's hand when she offered it. "How do you want it, darlin'?" he asked with a wicked leer down at her. "Slow and gentle, quick and rough... say the word and I'm at your service."

"So I see." She wiggled her hips, cradling his thickening arousal between her thighs. "You're pretty good there... wait, no. Let me turn over."

"Oh god, you want doggy style? You're killing me." He moved to sit back on his heels, rolling the condom on and watching lustfully as she turned over onto her stomach and pushing up onto hands and knees, casting a coquettish look at him over her shoulder.

"You're all talk. Show me some action," Carla demanded, and Jason moved, catching her hips in strong hands.

"Oh, honey, you're gonna get action. You better brace yourself." He made the first thrust slow, pressing steadily deeper inside her, not pulling back at all, just driving deep until his groin met her ass and he was fully seated.

Carla was panting, her knuckles white where she gripped the headboard, her back bowed as she pushed her ass back to meet Jason's penetration.

"Oh fuck, yes," she gasped, and then yelled his name loudly as he pulled halfway out and then slammed roughly back in again.

"Come on," Jason demanded, setting up a fast, steady rhythm of thrusts, dropping one hand around Carla's hip to feel between her legs, flick his fingertips roughly over her clit. "Let me feel you coming, darlin'. I want to feel you."

It wasn't long before he got his wish, Carla's small body convulsing in his grip as she clamped down on him, hoarse cries spilling from her lips. The strong tugging of her internal muscles on his cock had him just about seeing stars, the sensation just too much to take. He stilled, pressed deep inside her, and closed his eyes, letting her draw the orgasm out of him long and slow.

“Fuuuuuck,” he said finally, placing one hand at the small of Carla’s back to steady her as he pulled out slowly, making sure the condom stayed in place.

“What a fuck it was, too,” Carla agreed breathlessly, collapsing into a boneless heap on the mattress as Jason climbed off the bed and staggered off to the bathroom. His knees were shaking as he disposed of the condom and washed his hands; going back into the bedroom he flopped down beside Carla on the mattress.

“Damn, girl,” was all he said. Smiling, she wiggled closer and nestled her head on his shoulder, content to just lay with him in comfortable, sated silence.

She must have drifted off to sleep, because the next thing she knew she was waking up as Jason slid out of bed.

"Hm?" Carla blinked muzzily at him, wondering why he was putting his clothes on until she looked past him and saw that the sky outside the window was beginning to darken.

"I need to head back. Aunt Rose will be wondering what's happened to me." Pulling his shirt over his head, he stooped to kiss her. "When do we start investigating?"

Sitting up, pulling the sheet around her, she eyed him as he sat down on the edge of the bed to pull his boots on. "I want to make contact with a journalist I know. I know he was looking into the disappearance of those three boys a few months ago, and their connection to Julia Bulridge. I'd like to hear his take on things now, considering the events of the last couple of days."

"Sounds good," Jason nodded in agreement. "When will you talk to him?"

"He's a night owl; I'll give him a call this evening. Will you be able to come by tomorrow? I have a client coming in at nine, but I'm free after ten."

"Sure. Maybe I can make you some decent coffee." His eyes twinkled as he smiled down at her; she grabbed for a pillow and whacked him with it, laughing.

“Get out of here! Go take care of Rose.”

Jason fended the pillow off with a chuckle, flung himself full-length atop of Carla and pinning her down, trapping her face between his hands for a long, sensual kiss.

“Until tomorrow, beautiful,” he murmured at last, lifting his head. She smiled up at him, the heavy-lidded smile of a well-satisfied woman, and Jason needed another kiss before he could let her go.

Chapter Twelve

The impound lot wasn't far from Carla's house, just a couple of blocks. Obviously her terrorized school buddy had done her bidding and called ahead, because the lot manager was very eager to hand Jason's rental car keys back. Driving it over to the rental company's office in town, he paid for the extra day's hire without quibbling and accepted their offer of a ride to wherever he was headed.

Rose seemed exhausted when Jason arrived back at her house. Friends had long since filled her freezer with meals, but she only shook her head when he pressed her to eat. Eventually he managed to convince her to have some soup, since she needed to eat something to take her medication with.

"There's no point in this," she grumbled, washing the pills down with a few sips of water. "I'm dying, the pills aren't going to change that."

It was hard for him to hear her talk like that, Rose the indomitable, the one who had never backed down, never taken a backward step despite the years of abuse from her husband and her son, never allowed the Hunters to push Jason and his mother around.

"They're just to make you more comfortable," he said finally, taking the glass from her shaking hand.

"A stiff bourbon would do the job a lot better." She pushed herself to her feet, waving him away when he moved to assist her. "I know, I know, I can't have one. Not yet, anyway."

"Not yet?"

"Doc Walters says when the time gets close, he'll take me off the medication and I can have whatever I like. I'm got an expensive bottle of champagne in the cooler, and a packet of cigarettes." She sounded gleeful, like a teenager plotting a wild night of escape from parental authority.

"Aunt Rose, you haven't smoked since I was a child," Jason shook his head. "You'll cough your lungs up."

She smiled at him, a frail shadow of the strong, vibrant woman she had once been. No blood relation, she was still the only family he had apart from his mom and stepfather, or at least the only one he would acknowledge. The mere thought of losing her made his heart ache.

"There are worse ways to go, Jason," she said, and walked slowly down the hallway to her bedroom, her cane tapping a soft plunk-plunk as she went. "Good night, dear," her voice floated softly in the air behind her. "Sleep well."

Jason sat quietly for a while, staring out into the darkness through the window. Eventually he sighed and got up, heading to the kitchen to reheat the casserole he'd pulled from the freezer and tried to persuade his aunt to eat. He needed a meal himself, and he might as well eat it as throw it out.

After his solitary supper, he fished out his phone and did a little bit of searching and scrolling, wishing that Rose was technologically minded enough to own a computer. His phone screen was just too small to do any more than look up major news articles, and there were very few of those that even mentioned Woodvale, never mind covered in detail any missing persons reports. Perhaps he'd buy himself a laptop tomorrow; he probably needed a computer if he was going to help Carla research the disappearances.

Picking up his empty plate, he headed for the kitchen to wash up before going to his room. Sitting on the bed, looking around, he was transported back to his teenage years by the room's décor, unchanged since he left to go to college. There were flags and ribbons from his sporting achievements almost covering the wall opposite the bed, a shelf of his old schoolbooks still above the desk at which he'd spent many long hours slaving over his homework.

Considering the books, Jason went over to look and after a few minutes turned up an old exercise book with only a few pages used. Tearing them out and tossing them in the trash, he found a pencil in the desk drawer and settled down to make some notes. Heading each page with the name of one of the missing persons, beginning with Carla's mother, he filled in each page with everything he knew about the cases so far.

Slowly tapping the pencil tip on the last page, he considered what he knew about Julia Bulridge's disappearance. The only one of the missing persons who'd ever been seen again, she'd been silenced before she could tell what she knew, he was certain of it. He still had an awful lot of unanswered questions, starting with why she'd fled the relative safety of his car when she'd seemed very certain there were dogs in the woods hunting her.

It just didn't make sense. Yes, he was a stranger, but he'd helped her, told her he was going to get her medical treatment.

And, Jason thought, the last thing he'd done before Julia disappeared was call the police.

It seemed almost inconceivable, but had Julia run because she was afraid of somebody at the police station?

The tap of his pencil grew slower, and finally stopped. That was only speculation, Jason told himself, even if his instincts were absolutely screaming at him about Sheriff McCarthy. He had no evidence to support his hunch, and Julia fleeing his car right after he called the police could be coincidence. The car had been stopped, after all, and she could hardly have bailed out while it was still moving. She might have run no matter who he'd called.

Still, his phone call to the police was part of the timeline of Julia's death. He scribbled down verbatim as much of the conversation as he could recall. Maybe Carla could use her leverage with Floyd to get a recording or transcript of the call. It might even have the sound of Julia opening the car door in the background, a sound Jason had missed when it actually happened. The point during the conversation at which she had made her escape might tell them something.

Flipping to the back of the exercise book, he made a list of questions to ask Carla, and then a selection of keywords to search once he got his hands on a proper computer.

An unconscious smile crossed his face as he thought of Carla. Meeting her was an unexpected, though delightful, surprise. Sex with her had been better than he'd had in a long time… maybe ever. He couldn't remember ever having a partner so unapologetically sensual, whose desires meshed so perfectly with his own.

He was hard again just thinking about her. With a sigh, he set the pencil down and rose to his feet. Time to shower, and get some sleep. At least he wasn't likely to spend all night awake thinking things over in an endless loop. His years in the Rangers had taught him to shut his mind down when he needed to, to compartmentalize and grab sleep whenever he could get it.

Jason woke from a sound sleep with a jerk, instantly alert. The room was dark, but not pitch black; the drapes over the window were thin and let in a little diffuse light. Moonlight, he thought, lying completely still and listening, every sense straining to determine what it was that had woken him.

There.

The faintest of creaks. A footstep out in the great room.

And he didn't have so much as a knife.

There was, however, a baseball bat in the corner. A relic from his high school years. Easing silently from the bed, he curled his fingers around the worn grip, lifting the bat soundlessly as he moved on the balls of his feet to the door.

Another creak, this time closer. Whoever was out there would have to pass Jason to get to Aunt Rose's room, and that wasn't happening, not on his watch. Flinging his door wide, he leaped out into the hallway with a snarl on his lips.

Glass shattered and a scream rent the night.

"Jason! What the hell?" Aunt Rose stood, hand clutched to her throat, just an outline in the dim light cast by the nightlight plugged into the outlet in the hallway. Milk pooled around her feet.

"Oh my God." Horrified, he froze. "Don't move!" She wasn't wearing slippers, would cut her feet on the shattered glass.

“Is that your baseball bat?” Rose sounded scandalized as he hastily retreated into his room, dropping the bat back in the corner before grabbing his boots and yanking them on.

“Too much hassle to carry a gun across international borders, so yes. It’s the only weapon I had to hand,” he admitted, going back out to her and lifting her carefully off her feet. He was horrified at how little she weighed now; she seemed nothing more than a husk of skin and bone.

“Well, I must say I’m glad. You might have shot me!” Rose said indignantly.

“Don’t be ridiculous,” he scoffed. “I’ve never shot anyone I didn’t fully intend to.”

“Is that meant to be comforting?” she demanded, but she laughed as he carried her back to her bed. “Get me a wet cloth, Jason, there’s milk on my feet. I’m not putting them into bed like this.”

“Yes, Aunt Rose.” He obeyed her instructions dutifully, wiping her feet with the damp washcloth before going back to the kitchen and fetching her another glass of milk.

"Did you really think someone was breaking into the house?" Rose asked as he set the glass down on her nightstand, and Jason sighed.

"Yes," he said baldly.

"But why?" Her brow furrowed with confusion. "I've got nothing worth stealing."

"It's not about that." He sat down on the edge of her bed, careful not to bump her. "Something weird is going on in this town, and I'm afraid I stumbled right into the middle of it with poor Julia Bulridge. I think someone's worried that she was able to tell me something before she died."

"Tell you what?"

"I've no idea, because she didn't tell me anything. Someone thinks she might have done, though. Something that could point in their direction."

"And this is why they tried to arrest and silence you. Which means... they are in the police department. Or have influence there. Oh, Jason."

He tried to smile, but he'd already decided he wasn't going to sugar-coat things for Rose. Whatever time she had left was measured in days and weeks rather than months and years; he prayed he could keep trouble from her door, but he feared his arrival was going to seriously disrupt her peace. He said as much, and she reached out to grab his hand, her grip surprisingly strong considering her frailty.

"Trouble or not, I'd rather have you here, Jason. I'm glad you've come."

"I am too," he said, leaning over to kiss her cheek. "I'm not leaving you alone. So either we both go or we both stay; you choose, Aunt Rose. One phone call for a private jet, I promised you."

Her jaw set in a way he knew all too well; she might be no blood relation to him, but he saw that stubborn jut in the mirror when he was feeling particularly mulish.

"I'll not be chased out of my home. I want to die here, where I've been happy. Where my memories are."

"Anyone tries to chase you out, they'll have me to reckon with," Jason promised.

"And your trusty baseball bat?" Her faded eyes twinkled at him. "You do know I have a gun, don't you?"

His jaw dropped.

"Your mother and I took shooting lessons together, many years ago. I probably couldn't even hold it any more. Look in the bottom drawer." She gestured at her nightstand.

It was a Walther PPK/S, and Jason suspected it might be older than he was, but it was in perfect condition, clean and lightly oiled. A box of .380 ACP rounds was nestled into the lockbox beside it.

"You watched too many Bond movies," he accused.

"Always loved me a good action flick." Rose took a sip of her milk and lay back against her pillows wearily. "Take it, Jason. I have the alarming feeling you might need it."

Closing the lockbox, he tucked it under his arm before leaning to kiss her forehead. "Get some sleep, Aunt Rose."

"You too," she murmured, closing her eyes. "Oh, and Jason?" she said as he rose to leave. "Invite Carla for dinner tomorrow."

There was nothing he could say but "Yes, Aunt Rose."

Closing the door on her pleased smile, he went to clean up the mess of shattered glass and spilled milk in the hallway before taking the lockbox back to his room and disassembling the gun to check it. It was in perfect working order, and being a small, neat gun, fit perfectly in his jacket pocket. Under Idaho law, he didn't even need a license to carry it concealed.

Was he escalating things, carrying a gun, he wondered? Checking that it wasn't discernible in his jacket pocket, he took it back out, slowly loaded the seven-round magazine.

I've never been a fan of bringing a knife to a gunfight. Indeed, he'd been accused before of going for overkill in the weapons stakes -- not that his commanding officers had ever complained about the results he got. The little Walther was no machine gun or semi-automatic rifle, but he was under no illusions. If he needed more than the seven rounds the Walther carried, the situation was FUBAR and his odds of survival were approaching zero no matter what weapon he might be carrying.

Sleep was in short supply for Jason that night. When his aunt's respite care nurse arrived early in the morning, he was already up, making pancakes and bacon in the kitchen and considering his options. The Barclays had told him six people had gone missing in five months; he wanted to know if there'd been any other mysterious disappearances since Carla's mother four years ago.

Asking the police was obviously not an option, so he needed to go to the only other people in town who might have the information and be willing to share. Woodvale's newspaper, unfortunately, was one of many local businesses owned by his uncle. He doubted anyone employed there was going to be helpful, but their archives should be public. And, with any luck, digital.

Time to go buy himself a laptop, he decided, and popped his head around the door to Aunt Rose's room to tell her he was going out for a while and ask if she wanted anything. Lying in bed with an IV running into her arm, she only shook her head, obviously not even feeling well enough to offer him a smile.

On his way out the door, Jason’s somber mood was immediately improved as he saw Carla’s car pull up. She stepped out and grinned across at him.

“Hey. Going somewhere?”

“Computer shopping. Reading everything on my phone screen is driving me mad.”

“Want a ride?”

“Always.” He gave her a dirty grin, and she laughed.

“To the mall, you filthy beast.”

“That was what I meant!” he claimed virtuously, and completely untruthfully, as he slid into the passenger seat.

Chapter Thirteen

Carla put the car into Drive, chuckling and shaking her head. Jason's irrepressible charm could cheer up even the darkest of moods.

"So, what brought you up here?" he asked as she pulled out onto the main road. "Since you didn't come in, I take it you wanted to see me rather than my aunt?"

"I thought you might like to take a road trip with me," she said.

"Yeah? Where to?"

"Redstone Creek." She named the nearest town, which in northern Idaho meant a sixty-mile round trip.

"I've no objection to buying a laptop there instead of here, but is there a particular reason you want to go?" Jason pressed lightly.

"Research. I spent most of last night going through the Woodvale Gazette's archives and I've identified several other unexplained disappearances in the last six years, apart from my mother and the spate in the last few months."

"Ah, you're ahead of me. That was my plan once I picked up the laptop."

She darted a sideways glance at him, nodded in appreciation that he was apparently on a similar wavelength to her. "Got me wondering if it was just Woodvale. As it happens, that journalist friend I mentioned is an old schoolfriend who works for the Redstone Advertiser. When I called to ask some questions, he got very quiet, then said he'd like to meet in person to talk about it."

"Does my uncle have any stake in the Redstone Advertiser?" Jason asked point blank.

"No." She smiled tightly at his sigh of relief. "But the owner is a known associate of his.

They've done business together plenty of times in the past, they're both members of the same clubs. Walt Jackson."

Jason shrugged ignorance.

"Walt has the same sort of influence in Redstone Creek that Philip Hunter has in Woodvale."

"Oh, that's just terrific."

A sharp, humourless chuckle escaped her at the sarcasm in his tone. "And the Redstone Advertiser doesn't have online archives accessible to the general public beyond the last twelve months. My friend will help us out, I think, but we need to protect him as a source. Which means meeting him on his lunch break, somewhere out of the way."

"Good thing you picked me up, then," Jason said. "Just in case."

"Just in case what?" Confused, she took her eyes off the road briefly to frown at him.

"Just in case he's dirty, and you become the next statistic."

“Whoa,” Carla said when she got her breath back. “Pessimist much?”

“Realist,” he corrected. “I don’t understand what’s going on here, Carla, but one thing’s definitely clear; this is dirty business. Someone killed Julia Bulridge and tried to pin it on me simply because they were afraid she might have told me something, and they wanted me silenced. If you think they’d hesitate to make you disappear, you’re not being paranoid enough. Do you have a gun?”

“Yes,” she said immediately, but she could feel the guilty flush staining her neck.

“And where is it?” he asked remorselessly.

“In my gun safe at home.” She kept her eyes on the road ahead; she didn’t need to see his cynical sideways glance. “Okay, okay. I’ll get it out when I get home, keep it close. What about you, do you have a gun?”

“Yes,” he said, surprising her, “but I wouldn’t mind stopping by a gun supply store and picking up a holster for it. I’m not particularly keen on carrying it in my pocket. Might pick up something with a bit more range to it, as well.”

"Like a hunting rifle?"

From the corner of her eye, she saw Jason's shrug. "Since I don't think my preferred model of machine gun is available outside the military, sure. A hunting rifle."

"A machine gun might be overkill," she pointed out, half-laughing. He didn't say anything, and she found herself wondering what sort of action he'd seen in his years with the Rangers. A decade, or near enough, she figured, and one thing she knew about the Rangers was that they were always sent where the action was hottest. Afghanistan for sure, she guessed, and any number of other trouble spots, several of which he probably would never admit to having been in at all because the US military had never officially been there.

"Tell me about Guàlize," she requested, in lieu of asking him about the military service he almost certainly couldn't discuss. "You said something about knowing the President?"

"The President-elect. It's a long story, but my former captain in the Rangers is married to the incoming president's daughter. Captain

McAuley was asked to assist with setting up a paramilitary, anti-drug trafficking task force, helping the Guàlizeans train elite troops. I was coming to the end of my current term of enlistment and he called me and offered me a job." Jason paused, and Carla was fairly sure he was mentally editing his story for civilian consumption. "I'd been in action with him in Guàlize once. Liked the place, and the people, and the money they offered was excellent. Plus, a lot less chance of getting shot at."

Carla was fairly sure the United States had never been officially involved in any action in Guàlize, a friendly South American nation, in the last decade. She was also sure Jason wasn't going to elaborate, so she didn't push. "So, you're a training instructor now? What's your specialty?"

"Woodland warfare." He smiled as he looked out of the window, at the vast pine forests on either side of the road they drove along. "Different woods down there to the ones I grew up with, of course. Tropical rainforests. But the basic principles are the same."

"There are still things out there that will eat you if you give them the opportunity?" Carla teased.

"Yup." He chuckled. "Instead of bears, wolves and mountain lions, it's jaguar, caiman and piranha."

Her shudder was entirely unfeigned.

"I won't tell you about the bugs and snakes, huh?"

"Definitely not! I might live in a small town but the emphasis is on town. I'm an urban creature."

"Well, you'd like Guàlize City. It's absolutely stunning. Lots of gorgeous architecture, both colonial era and modern, and some amazing architectural sites close by to visit. And the food!" He brought one hand to his lips, kissed his fingertips in a chef's kiss. "Best street food in the world, bar none. My mouth's watering just thinking about my favorite quesadilla stall."

"Oh man," Carla said wistfully. "I'd kill for some decent Latin street food. There isn't a

Mexican restaurant for two hundred miles. Not so much as a freaking Taco Bell."

"I'll cook you some," Jason said. He grinned at her shocked face. "I'm a good cook. Trust me."

"With my life? Sure. In my kitchen? Dunno about that, buddy."

They drove on, chatting easily, and Carla thought privately how very easy it was to feel comfortable around Jason Hunter.

Arriving in Redstone Creek, Carla pulled into the carpark in front of the office supply store. "Best place to pick up a laptop, I think," she said, and Jason nodded, sliding easily out of the car.

"You need anything?" he asked.

"Oh, I'm coming in." She grinned across at him, locking the car. "I confess to a bit of a weakness for office supplies. I'm a hoarder of nice notebooks."

He didn't even made a snide remark, which lifted him yet another notch in Carla's estimation. Hot, funny, charming and considerate, she thought; how the heck had he not been snapped up yet?

Jason picked up a mid-range laptop, a mouse and a satchel to carry them around in. Carla had a whole basketful of stationery when they met back up at the checkouts, but he didn't say anything, just followed her back to the car once they'd both paid.

The gun store was only a couple of blocks away, and here Jason seemed to come alive, chatting knowledgeably with the store clerk, who obviously picked him as military from the first moment. Jason took his time over selections, picking up ammunition, a shoulder-rig holster for the handgun he took from his jacket pocket, and then selecting a surprisingly inexpensive hunting rifle, though the clerk tried to point him to a high-end one.

"I'm not looking to make shots at half a mile," Jason said gruffly, examining the rifle carefully. "It'll be plenty accurate at a couple hundred yards." He picked up a night-vision scope for it, though, and Carla had to wonder what scenarios he was envisaging where he might need it.

"I'll take that, too," Jason said as they set everything on the front counter.

Carla looked to see what he was pointing at, gaped at the pump-action shotgun the clerk was taking from a display case. “What do you think we’re going to be dealing with?” she asked in an undertone.

“Hopefully, nothing.” Jason nodded at the shotgun shells the clerk offered. “Four boxes, please.” He turned to look at Carla. “But if I’m wrong… the bad guys are going to find out the hard way they should never have fucked with me.”

His jaw had set hard, and there was a light in his blue eyes she hadn’t seen before. This was the professional soldier standing before her, Carla realized, the Ranger preparing for his mission. Arming for a war he didn’t want to have to fight.

They locked everything except Jason’s handgun in the trunk, swung by the diner to pick up some sandwiches and coffee to go, before driving to the quiet park where Carla’s friend had asked to meet. He was sitting on a bench overlooking the creek which gave Redstone Creek its name, watching some small children throwing bread at the ducks under the watchful eyes of their parents.

“Barry Hillsum. It’s been a minute,” she said cheerfully, sitting down beside him.

“And you’ve only got prettier,” Barry said, with a sideways glance at her through his thick glasses and a sheepish grin. He’d always been the shy, nerdy type; they’d edited the Woodvale High school newspaper together. “Who’s your friend?” He frowned at Jason.

“Jason Hunter.”

Barry was already a pasty white; he turned almost green, bolting to his feet. “Hunter?”

“Sit down.” Carla made a soothing gesture. “He’s not one of them.”

“Technically, I am, since Philip’s my uncle,” Jason said, “but I think he’s a total scumbag, so if he’s your enemy, you can consider me solidly on your side.”

“He’s not my enemy.” Barry took a seat, eyeing Jason cautiously. “I’d rather he remain in total ignorance of my existence, though.”

“I have no intention of mentioning your name to anyone. Forgotten it already, in fact. Brian, wasn’t it?”

Barry's lips quirked slightly. "I think I like him," he murmured to Carla. "You trust him?"

"I do," she said.

"Good enough. You always were a straight arrow, Carla; I'm trusting you with this because I honestly don't know who else to turn to. My boss ordered me to not just discontinue investigating the story, but actively discourage anyone else from looking into it either, and something stinks."

"What story?" Carla had never seen Barry like this. He seemed jittery, nervous; looking around regularly and staring at anyone who even looked in their direction.

"You asked me about people who've disappeared around Redstone Creek in the last few years. End of last year, there was a high profile one; two young women who were supposed to be coming home from college for Christmas. They never got off their Greyhound."

"Names?" Jason asked quietly. He'd pulled a notepad from somewhere, sat with pencil poised over it.

"Emily Darnell and Sasha Thoms. Both twenty years old, both studying in Boise. By all accounts model students, close friends, nothing unusual about either of them. They were last seen at a rest stop about fifty miles from here, taking a bathroom break. The bus driver said they took their bags off the bus and didn't get back on even though they had tickets purchased through to Redstone Creek. The assumption was that they'd met someone they knew who'd offered to take them the rest of the way home, but nobody has been able to figure out who that was. They just vanished, seemingly into thin air."

"And being pretty young white women, it attracted media attention?" Carla asked, a little cynically.

"Emily Darnell's uncle is a state senator," Barry said.

Jason let out a soft whistle. "Okay, no wonder you said high profile."

Barry nodded at him. "He got the FBI involved, claimed he'd been a target of domestic terrorism threats and his enemies might have taken Emily. They turned over every damn rock between here and Boise, seemed like... and nothing. No trace of the girls."

"I don't get it," Carla said. "What's the point of your editor ordering you to kill the story? Something like this takes on a life of its own, garners national press interest."

"Not the story of those two. The story about the others."

Carla felt her eyebrows fly up. "What others?"

"The Darnell and Thoms case is probably the biggest thing ever to happen in Redstone Creek. But they're not the only disappearances. I've been working on this newspaper for seven years, and in that time, I've written up twenty missing-persons articles, from apparent teenage runaways to adults who left home looking for work and never contacted their families again. Now, I don't know if you know, but national statistics on missing persons show that between 89 to 92 per cent of missing persons are found, dead or alive, within the first year. Want to know how many of the Redstone Creek missing persons turned up?"

Carla shrugged. "Sure."

"None."

"I'm sorry." Jason leaned in, gaze intent. "You're saying that statistically, eighteen of those twenty should have been found, one way or another, but none ever have?"

"That's exactly what I'm saying." Barry met his eyes unflinching.

"Shit." Jason voiced what Carla was thinking. "That stinks to high heaven. Some of them should have turned up, even if it was as an identified body."

"Yup. I started collating information and talking to families - those who would talk. Most of them go a little white around the lips and refuse to even talk about it. Even Emily Darnell's uncle, I should point out. For a couple weeks after she and Sasha vanished, you couldn't turn on the TV without seeing his face. Then, he suddenly went all quiet. And since then, he's made some... let's call them, out of character moves, politically."

Carla blew out her cheeks. "Do you think Emily's disappearance was a warning?" she asked. "Change your policies, or next time, it'll be someone closer than a niece?"

“Maybe. He wouldn’t speak to me, so I’ve no way to test the theory. And even if someone did threaten him that way, who’s to say it was actually the person who took Emily? Could have been an opportunist, looking to make hay.” Barry spread his hands uncertainly. “All I know for sure is after I tried to get an interview with Senator Darnell, that’s when my editor stopped by my desk, demanded all my research, and told me the story was dead and I was to, and I quote, stop harassing grieving families.”

“Sweet Jesus,” Carla muttered, her head spinning.

“How long?” Jason asked after a couple of minutes of silence.

“Excuse me?” Barry frowned at him.

“You said you’ve been working on the paper for seven years and have covered twenty cases. Right from the start of your career? Is it possible these mysterious disappearances started even earlier?”

Barry blinked a few times, licked his lips. Pulled a notebook of his own out and started paging through it, obviously consulting his notes. “It’s… consistent,” he said. “Two or three a year. So… yes. It could have started earlier.”

“Could you look into it?” Carla asked. “Quietly. Of course. Just a look through the newspaper archives. The Redstone Creek Advertiser’s aren’t publicly available without registering an account and paying a fee, and I’m reluctant to put my name on anything at this point.”

“Understandable.” Barry nodded sharply, and then he ripped a piece of paper from his pad, scribbled something on it and passed it over. “Do you have a VPN and a burner email?”

“No, but I will by tonight,” Carla said after a moment of stunned silence.

“When you do, email me on that email address. I’ll send you a summary of what I have so far, with names and dates. Don’t put anything into a search engine unless your VPN is running.” With a nod and a brief pat on her arm, Barry rose to his feet. “I need to get back to work. I’ve got a school musical to report on this afternoon. Riveting stuff.”

She could see how quietly angry he was, how much he longed to be chasing after the real story. Finding answers and getting closure for the families of the missing. "Be careful, Barry," she said softly. "Watch your back. And thank you."

"If there's a story here," he said, ever the journalist, "I want it. I'll quit my job, write it, and sell it to the New York Times."

"If we figure it out, the story's yours," Carla promised, and he nodded once more before turning on his heel and walking away.

Chapter Fourteen

It was a quiet drive back to Woodvale, Carla and Jason both lost in their own thoughts. Finally, Jason looked across at Carla, who had spent much of the drive with her lower lip caught between her teeth, nibbling on it as her brain obviously worked furiously.

"You said you'd looked into the newspaper archive in Woodvale and found 'some' disappearances. How many total, and how far back did you go?"

"I only went back five years," Carla said. "Which is as far as I could go without having to create a paid account or go to the library or the newspaper offices."

"Which might be inadvisable," Jason murmured.

"Mm hm. But in answer to your question, it was more than twenty, in five years. Maybe thirty. I assumed some of them had turned up, though. And what about that thing Barry said - some of the ones he'd written up were people who'd supposedly gone away looking for work, and never contacted their families again. I'm sure there are people like that from Woodvale. I can think of at least one, actually. I just assumed he'd left his wife, but... now I think about it... he adored her, and their kids. I never quite believed he'd run out on them, and I know she never accepted it. He was going to head up north, try to find work in the oilfields in Alaska."

"And now you're thinking, if we investigated, we'd find he never got to Alaska at all?"

"I don't think he ever left Idaho. Along with my mom, and all the others. Jesus, Jason." She took her eyes off the road briefly, shot a glance at him which was decidedly afraid. "What have we stumbled into?"

He didn't know. It was far, far outside even his extensive experience in the military. People died in war, yes, but there was a reason for it, a body, an investigation. Not just complete disappearance and radio silence. Not literally dozens of people, including the niece of a state senator.

He kept coming back to that one. Looking down at the notepad on his lap, Emily Darnell's name written at the top of a page and circled heavily.

"When you email Barry," he said, "ask if anyone's gone missing in Redstone Creek since the Darnell girl and her friend."

"Why?" Carla asked.

"Because I think they were a mistake. Someone being cocky. Think about it. Everyone else who has disappeared, it's been the sort of people who do disappear. Troubled kids. Old folks with dementia - no disrespect intended to your mother, Carla."

"None taken." Carla's brow furrowed. "And people who were in between places, who weren't easily missed. Those who left for work, or college, and just never came back."

"Exactly." Jason tapped a finger on Emily Darnell's name. "She and Sasha were coming back from college. They were expected; they were missed. They brought attention that must have been unwanted. So either they aren't part of the pattern - it's a different perpetrator, maybe someone who preys on pretty young women and took his chance - or someone fucked up. In which case, disappearances in Redstone Creek would logically dry up for a while at least, while whoever is behind it lays low for a bit."

"Or it's part of the pattern but had a different purpose. Like Barry theorized. Leverage on the uncle."

"Argh." Jason gripped his head. "This is too complicated. Give me a nice simple murderous drug warlord any day."

Carla chuckled, but there was no humor in the sound. "And I have to point out that if it's a different perp, the disappearances might well dry up too. Whoever is responsible for the other disappearances choosing to lie low until the focus moves off Redstone Creek."

"Shit." She was right, he realized. "So, they... moved operations to Woodvale? Which explains the sudden spate in the last few months."

"It does. Their hunting area shrank in size." Carla's fingers flexed on the wheel. "I reckon," she said after a few more minutes of silence, "if we track the disappearances, we're going to find it works out right about one a month. Pretty evenly spaced out."

"Why?" Jason slapped his hand on the dash in frustration. "That's what I don't understand, why? There's no pattern to the victims. Young, old, male, female. Black, white, Latino. Everything I know about serial killers says they have a preferred type of victim. The Darnell girl could be some sort of power play, but none of the other victims fit that pattern."

"It rules out any sort of human trafficking or sexual motive," Carla said. "Even going more far-fetched, if you were kidnapping people to harvest organs for the black market or something, you're not going to take people like Julia Bulridge or my mom."

"What does that leave?" Jason asked, coming up blank.

"I don't know." Carla chewed on her lip for a while as the endless forests whizzed by outside the car windows. "A thrill killer?" she said finally. "Someone who gets off on seeing the lights go out?"

It was the only answer which made any kind of sense, but it still didn't ring true to Jason. "One person?" he said doubtfully. Considering everything else they'd discovered, not to mention the obvious desire of the sheriff's department not to have anyone looking into the disappearances, it didn't add up. Not even his uncle, with all his clout, had the influence and cash to buy off that many people.

"I don't know, Jason." Carla sounded almost despairing. "I just don't know."

They were still missing some vital piece of the puzzle, surely. Jason just couldn't comprehend what it might be. He thought again of Julia Bulridge, wishing desperately she'd trusted him enough to tell him something before she fled the car into the darkness.

Looking down at the notepad on his lap, he remembered something else he wanted to check into. Flipping to a fresh page, he scribbled.

“What are you writing?” Carla asked.

“Reminding myself to find out what Sheriff Thomas McCarthy used to do in the Navy.”

“What’s that got to do with anything?” She sounded puzzled.

“Probably nothing. I just like to know who I’m up against.”

“Do you have sources? Otherwise I can probably reach out to a friend of mine who’s with the FBI now. I was planning to anyway.”

“I can get the information.” Jason planned to email his old commanding officer. Colonel Brody Cullane was a source he regularly reached out to when he needed information to help him in his work in Guàlize; he might be off-the-books here but he was pretty sure the Colonel would still come through, especially in a small matter like looking up a former sailor’s service records. While he thought about it, he pulled out his phone, brought up the email program and typed out a rapid message.

There was no immediate response, but he’d hardly expected one. Putting the phone away, he said; "You didn't mention you had a buddy in the FBI."

"A law school buddy." Carla nodded. "I sent her copies of the motel footage which provided your alibi. Just in case. This sort of thing wouldn't be her area - she works financial crimes out of the Buffalo office these days - but she'd start the ball rolling if I hadn't followed up, and she'll put me in touch with people who'll listen once we've assembled something worth looking at."

"Gotcha." They were almost back to Woodvale now. "Would you mind swinging by the grocery store before dropping me back at Rose's?"

"Sure. I could probably do with picking up something for dinner, anyway."

"As to that, Aunt Rose told me to invite you to dinner. So, if you're willing to risk my cooking - I thought I'd make some of that Guàlizean street food I promised you. My version of it, at least."

"How could I possibly turn down an invitation like that?"

She was utterly gorgeous when she smiled, and Jason felt the lust he'd been working on suppressing all day making its way to the surface. "We could make a stop at your place too."

"Yeah?" She shot him a sidelong glance. "What for?"

"I think you know what for."

"In that case." She indicated and turned off the main road onto a side street. "We'd best go there first. Otherwise the groceries might be sitting in the car too long."

Despite the uncertainty and concern he felt about the missing people, Jason felt a warm glow of contentment as Carla drove him back to Rose's house. He'd called Rose from Carla's house earlier to let her know he wouldn't be back for a while yet; she'd told him cheerfully there was a movie she planned to watch on TCM that afternoon and not to worry in the slightest. Which made him feel a lot less guilty about spending two hours in bed with Carla.

After making love (twice) they'd sat in bed with their laptops and researched, comfortable in being nude together while they worked. Carla had printed off some single-page annual calendars for the last five years and they'd carefully marked off every disappearance they could find in a hundred-mile radius around Woodvale, referring to the list Barry had emailed her and using different colored pens to code where the person vanished from.

When they'd finished, they sat back and looked at the sheets. Carla was correct; the disappearances were almost exactly at one a month. On the few occasions the pattern was broken, more than one person had gone missing at once, like Emily Darnell and Sasha Thoms or the Whitton brothers and Mark Martin, who the Barclays had told him about on his first night back in Woodvale.

“It's one disappearance a month, but I can't see any pattern,” Jason said finally. “It's on different days of the month and different days of the week.”

Carla was chewing on her lip again, in that way he'd come to realize meant she was thinking hard. She reached out and tapped a finger slowly on a symbol on one of the calendars, one they hadn't put there.

“The full moon?” Jason asked blankly. It was pure coincidence the calendars she’d printed had the moon cycle symbols on them, he suspected.

“Almost all the disappearances occur three or four days before the full moon. Julia Bulridge is the furthest out, nine days before full moon.”

“So, what?” He half-laughed. “You think there’s some sort of twisted Satanic or dark Wiccan cult out there kidnapping people to use as human sacrifices in a full moon ritual?”

“Hearing you say it out loud, it sounds utterly ridiculous, but... can you come up with a more likely scenario?”

Carla leaned back against her pillows and watched as Jason spread the printed pages out on the bed, scanning the dates, looking for other patterns. Watching the muscles play under the tan skin of his shoulders and chest was a treat; she felt guilty for getting distracted sexually considering the gravity of what they were researching, but she'd never felt more alive than right at that moment.

"I think it's time we contacted my FBI buddy," she said finally, when Jason just shook his head slowly in answer to her question. "She can track down whoever was looking into the Darnell girl's disappearance, see if maybe they'll talk to us. Because even if there might be a different motive there with the state senator, fact is, she and her friend still fit the pattern of someone disappearing just before a full moon - and there are no other disappearances that month."

"That we know about," Jason pointed out, and Carla nodded, conceding the point. If they could just get the FBI to look at the data they'd gathered, though, they could bring far greater resources to bear.

Getting out of bed, she slipped her robe on and gathered the pages to take to the scanner. She'd email them to her FBI friend now, and to Marcus Devereaux at the DA's office.

Jason got out of bed too, pulling his clothes on, his reluctant expression telling her he'd much rather be spending the rest of the afternoon in bed too. They needed to go to the grocery store, though, and then get back to Rose's.

Jason's phone chirped as he pulled on his pants, and he fished it from his pocket, tapped the screen and frowned. "Huh. Didn't expect that."

"What?" Carla turned from feeding the last page into the scanner.

"My old commanding officer did me a favor and looked up Sheriff McCarthy's Navy service record. He was a dog handler." Jason's face darked as he scrolled and read further. "He was dishonorably discharged. Accused of setting his service dog to attack an innocent civilian."

"That didn't come up when he was running for sheriff!" Carla stared at him, shocked. "Was he convicted?"

"Accused the dog of going rogue, from what this says. Accepted a dishonorable discharge rather than go to trial. Does the police department here have any dogs?"

"No, and I don't think McCarthy has a pet dog, either. Leastways, I've never seen him with one."

"Julia talked about dogs." Jason's gaze turned inward as he obviously remembered back to finding Julia Bulridge, cold and terrified in the rain and darkness. "She was scared out of her wits, said she could 'hear the dogs'."

"Did you hear anything?"

He shook his head, buttoning his shirt. "Nothing but the wind and the rain, which was pretty loud at that point."

Carla chewed her lip thoughtfully, but she couldn't see how it might be relevant. She hadn't heard any stories about dogs loose in the woods, and said so.

"Wolves?" Jason wondered.

"I mean, I'm sure they're out there. But Julia Bulridge spent years in Woodvale, and came from another small town in Idaho before that. In her younger days, she liked to hike and shoot. She knew the difference between dogs and wolves."

"Hm. Why don't you email Barry - ask if he's heard anything about dogs on the loose?"

"You got it." Firing off the email to her FBI friend copied to the DA, she quickly typed out another to Barry and sent that, too. There was no immediate response, so she left the laptop open while she dressed in skinny jeans and a scoop-necked tee, in a fiery red she knew looked great with her skin and hair. Catching Jason staring at her admiringly, she sent him a cheeky wink while she sat on the bed to put on her heeled ankle boots. "You should stop looking at me like that, or you won't have time to cook me dinner."

He laughed, and came over to take her in his arms and kiss her again, slow and lingering. "Whatever the hell is going on here, Carla," he said quietly, leaning his brow against hers, "I'm not sorry it's led me to you."

"Neither am I," she whispered back, and they stayed like that, leaning into each other, for a long, blissful moment of silence.

He didn't make her any promises, and she appreciated that. They both knew they were into something deep and dark, maybe darker than even he had seen, despite his experience of war. That dozens of people had disappeared without trace, and whoever had made them disappear was doing a damn good job of covering their tracks. And that, whether they liked it or not, Carla and Jason were on their radar.

The only choice they really had was to figure out what was going on, and who was doing it. Because leaving town, as Jason had suggested, wasn't an option. Not when Carla was sure the disappearances weren't going to stop.

She quite simply couldn't live with that on her conscience.

Chapter Fifteen

They stopped by the grocery store to pick up some supplies before Carla drove Jason back to Rose's house. The rain had started again, after a mostly dry day, and they hurried up the steps, Carla's arms full of grocery bags and Jason loaded down with the long gun carry case, laptop computer and bag of ammunition.

The front door was open.

Just a few inches ajar, but Carla hesitated on the threshold. Dark was falling, and she didn't think Rose was the type to leave her door open. Maybe the care nurse hadn't closed it properly when she left?

"Jason," she said softly.

“What is it?” Coming up the steps behind her, he took in her body language, saw the open door and stiffened. “It wasn’t locked?”

“It was open.”

He hissed between his teeth. Set the laptop bag down against the side of the porch, reached under his jacket to draw his pistol. “Stand aside, Carla. Rose would never leave her door open.”

She swallowed, her heart suddenly hammering a thunderous rhythm, moved over to let him pass. He eased the long gun case off his shoulder, leaned it against the side of the porch. Set the ammunition bag down too.

“Press yourself against the wall. Sideways on. Small target,” he breathed it very softly against her cheek, waited until she obeyed before moving forward in a sudden blur of motion, almost too fast for her to follow, kicking the door open and springing through it, gun at the ready in his hand.

Carla stood, holding her breath, listening hard. She could hear nothing, though, not even Jason's footsteps as he moved through the house.

He was back in under a minute, expression grim. "Rose isn't here," he clipped out, grasping her elbow to urge her quickly inside, stopping to grab everything he'd dropped. Slamming the door closed, he twisted the lock.

"What do you mean, not here? Where's she gone?"

"No idea."

Jason's face was drawn, grim, his mouth set in a hard line. He moved to the windows, quickly jerking the drapes across, before switching on the light.

Carla looked around, wondering what was causing the furrows in his brow to deepen further. Nothing looked out of place as far as she could see. There were several occasional tables in the front room with lamps and knick-knacks, some of which would surely have been disturbed if there was any kind of trouble.

"What are you seeing?" she asked.

“Aunt Rose’s purse.” Jason pointed to a large brown purse, on the floor beside a reclining easy chair. “And her phone.” A cellphone was lying on the coffee table, a basic one with a number keypad rather than a smartphone. “No way would she go anywhere without them.” He dropped to one knee, unzipping the long gun bag. “I don’t like this, Carla.”

“Maybe she was taken ill.” Carla tried to think of a good reason for Rose to be missing. “Picked up by an ambulance?”

“You got the number for the Barclays, next door? They’d know if that happened.” As she was dialling, Jason added “Of course, they’d have called me as soon as it did, so I doubt it.”

Mrs Barclay answered after a couple of rings. “Rose?” she said in response to Carla’s query. “No, I haven’t seen her since this morning. I popped over with some soup I’d made for lunch. Should I come over?”

“No,” Carla said quickly. “No, please stay home. Keep your drapes drawn.”

There was a brief silence, then Mr Barclay came on the line. “Young lady, I don’t like the sound of this. Where’s Rose? And Jason?”

“Jason’s here with me now. We don’t understand where Rose is; that’s why we’re calling. We got back to find her missing.”

Jason was moving through the house on silent feet, the shotgun in his hands, his eyes alert as he checked every room.

“Did you see anything this afternoon? A strange car outside on the street?” Carla asked hopefully.

“I’m sorry, Ms. Ramirez. We haven’t,” Barclay said, and she heard his wife agree in the background. “Should we call the police?” he asked, then laughed harshly. “Listen to me. Still believing in law and order.”

“I still believe in law and order, Mr. Barclay. It’s just that the sheriff of Woodvale apparently doesn’t. Don’t call the police - but do you have a pen and paper? I’m going to give you a couple of phone calls and ask you to call some other people for me. One of them is a friend of mine with the FBI.”

Jason, coming back into the room then, gave her an approving nod. “Your DA friend as well,” he said quietly, “and Barry.” He pulled out his own phone as Carla was reciting numbers and giving instructions to the Barclays, dialled a number.

Jason had wanted to avoid this step, but he no longer had a choice. “Sir,” he said when his boss, former Captain Jack McAuley, picked up the phone, “I believe I need a very large favour.”

“I probably owe you a few,” Jack answered easily. “What do you need?”

“Backup.”

There was a brief silence. “Rangers would be closer,” Jack said.

“I know, but asking them to operate on American soil will be opening a can of worms.”

“And Guàlizean troops will be better?”

Jason winced. “Plausibly deniable private mercenaries?” he tried.

“What in the absolute fuck is going on, Hunter?”

“I wish I knew,” Jason said honestly, “but I’m pretty sure that at least fifty people are dead, maybe more, and my Aunt Rose might be next. She’s missing.”

Jack knew exactly who Rose was, and what she meant to Jason. He’d eaten plenty of her care-package cookies. He spent a couple of seconds to curse, and then said crisply “I’ll have men on a plane tonight.”

“Have them come to Rose’s house. There’ll be a woman here, an attorney by the name of Carla Ramirez. She knows everything I do, probably more. She’ll fill them in.”

“And where will you be?” The foreboding in Jack’s voice said he knew exactly what Jason planned to do.

“I’m going to find Aunt Rose.”

Hanging up, he turned to face Carla, who had her hands on her hips, glaring at him. “No way am I sitting here while you go… where? You don't even know where to look!"

"I know where to start," Jason said.

"The sheriff's office? You'll be arrested the moment you walk in the door!"

He shook his head, a wry smile touching his lips. "No, I'm not that dumb. They won't have taken Rose there. Despite what I think of the sheriff, I don't think the whole department is corrupt. Your old school buddy seemed all right, if clueless. Word would spread."

"Then where?"

"Where it all started." Jason picked up the rifle he'd bought earlier that day, never more grateful for his own paranoia. "My uncle's house."

Carla stared at him, obviously trying to understand, and he tried to explain himself.

"Rose is Philip's mother. Follow the logic tree here, okay? I'm operating on the assumption that whoever took her has done it to force me to back off - or plans to lure me into a trap. Either way, she's a weapon against me."

"Right," Carla said with a slow nod. "I'm with you so far."

"Either my uncle doesn't know about it -- in which case, I can appeal to the fact that I think he might still love his mother, just a little bit, and try and get him to call in some favors to ensure she's safe -- or he does know about it, in which case, she's almost certainly been taken to his house."

Carla chewed on her lip as she mulled over his conclusions, and Jason thought she was about to use her sharp lawyer's mind to probably poke a thousand holes in his logic and enumerate a bunch of other solutions. Which he would have welcomed, because an innocent, logical explanation for where Rose was would be a huge relief.

Instead, she shook her head slowly. "You think he does know, don't you? You think he's involved in all this... whatever this filth is. And he's willing to use his own mother as a hostage to stop you from finding out."

"Yes," Jason said baldly.

"I'm definitely not staying here, then."

He blinked at her. “Come again?”

“They have to stop me too, Jason. And my mother’s already gone. There are no hostages they can use against me. If you leave me here, I’m a sitting duck.”

Her phone rang as he was staring at her, marshaling his arguments as to why she was wrong -- though he suspected arguing with a lawyer wasn’t going to end well for him. Carla fished her phone out and looked at it.

“Barry,” she said, and he nodded, waited for her to answer.

Carla tapped the button to put the phone on speaker, holding it out between them. “Hey, Barry,” she said.

Silence.

Carla’s gaze snapped from the phone up to meet Jason’s, sudden dread on her expression.

“Barry?” Jason said, thinking a male voice on the line might make whoever it was think twice. Assuming it wasn’t Barry, anyway.

"Just leave," a mechanically distorted voice said. "This is your only warning. Both of you. Get in the car and leave. Leave the state. Leave the country."

"Barry," Carla mouthed silently, anguish on her face. Jason shook his head, warning her not to say it.

"You already know I'm not going to do that," he said. "And you know why. Let Barry and Rose go, cut your losses. You leave. Because I'm coming for you."

The laugh sounded horrible through the distorting device the caller was obviously using. Like something from a horror movie. Carla pressed her free hand over her mouth. It was shaking, and the rage that welled up inside Jason was so deep, so brutal, it shocked him.

"Run," he said harshly. "Run, as fast as you can, and you'd better not ever fucking stop looking over your shoulder, asshole, because I'm coming for you. And you'd better believe Rangers catch what we're hunting." He stabbed his finger down on the screen to cut the call, took the phone from Carla and switched it off.

"What..." she said.

"It's literally a high-functioning tracking device. I don't think they're that hooked up, but I might be wrong. We leave them behind when we go. Computers, too."

Looking at the phone in her hand as though it were a poisonous snake, Carla placed it carefully on the coffee table. "Do you think that's how they got to Barry... they were tracking our phones?"

"No." Jason shook his head. "I think they were already watching him. He'd already asked too many questions. Remember, he said he'd been ordered to back off the story he was writing."

"Shit." She screwed her eyes shut, took a deep breath. "Do you think he's already dead?"

Her voice was very small, and Jason wanted to take her in his arms and hold her tight, promise he'd make everything alright. That he'd protect her and find Rose and Barry and everything would turn out okay.

But both of them knew that would be bullshit, so he didn't say it.

"You're right that you can't stay here," he said instead. "You should go home. And call as many friends as you can think of to meet you there. Your buddy the deputy, that DA friend of yours, anyone else you can think of with influence. Call them now, tell them to meet you there, and go. Tell them what Barry told you, tell them he's now missing. The more people who know, the safer you are; the less likely this can stay hidden."

"You're going to find them." Her voice shook, but she met his eyes squarely. "You're going to find them, Jason, and you're going to tell the FBI all about this yourself and we're going to bring whoever is doing this to justice."

"I am," he agreed, his voice steady.

He didn't add what he was silently thinking, but he was pretty sure Carla knew.

Or die trying.

Chapter Sixteen

"What do we do now?" Carla asked, watching Jason as he quietly and efficiently loaded himself up. He'd bought a pair of cargo pants and a hunting vest, both with lots of pockets; he changed into them and filled the pockets with ammunition now.

"Drop me off on Greens Road and go home," Jason said shortly. "Use your office landline to call all the folks we talked about, and anyone else you can think of."

Greens Road wasn't the road Philip Hunter lived off; Carla's brow furrowed as she considered the geography. It was at right angles to the Hunter property, she thought, and one side of it was all thick woods, through which Jason would be able to move unseen to get onto his uncle's land.

"You're not going to walk up and ring the doorbell, then?" she asked.

"Knocking on the front door is only a good tactic if you're going in with overwhelming force," Jason said dryly, "and since I don't see a handy SWAT team around here to back me up, I'm going for the sneak approach. I want to get the lay of the land."

They passed a police car going in the opposite direction at one point on the drive, and both held their breath for a long moment, peering in the mirrors.

"If he turns around, pull over immediately and I'll bail out," Jason said quietly, leaning forward to stare into the side mirror.

Carla's knuckles were white where she gripped the steering wheel. "We don't think the whole sheriff's department are dirty. Right?"

"Can't be. There's what, more than a dozen of them? And some of them must have been in the department before McCarthy came in, right?"

"A few," Carla agreed. "Deputy Cargill was an old-timer back in my schooldays; you must remember her. She was always the one called down to the school to deal with kids who got into deep shit. She's got kids there herself now; I can't imagine she'd be involved in whatever this shitshow is, but at the same time, how have none of them noticed?"

"You'd be surprised." Jason stopped watching the mirrors. "McCarthy strikes me as the kind of guy who compartmentalizes information. Everything on a need to know basis; if it's not your case, it's none of your business. Stomp hard a few times on people sticking their noses where he doesn't want them, it wouldn't take long for him to condition them to stop looking outside their own little boxes."

"You sound like you've had experience with that?" Carla glanced across at him.

"I was lucky in my commanding officers in the Rangers, but every now and then you cross paths with a unit who has a guy like that in charge." Jason grimaced. "They had a tendency to get killed in action… leaving the desk jockey who'd fucked them up that way alive to go on and fuck up another unit."

They were approaching the turning to Greens Road now, and as soon as Carla had made the turn, Jason said "Turn your lights off."

"Now I really hope that cop car didn't turn to follow us, because he's got a ready-made excuse to pull me over," Carla said, not joking in the slightest.

"He didn't turn. Nobody's been behind us for the last few minutes." Jason reached up and clicked the switch on the dome light, ensuring it wouldn't come on when he got out of the car. "Over here."

There were no streetlights here, and the houses on the built-up side of the road were widely spaced and set well back. No porch lights reached the dark, shadowed spot Jason had indicated.

Carla swallowed. "I'm scared," she said in a small voice.

"You're gonna be okay." Jason's voice was soft in the darkness. He put his hand against her cheek, leaned in so his brow touched hers. “Go home, turn all the lights on, call friends and get them to come over and stay with you.”

“I’m not scared for me, I’m scared for you!”

He made a soft, huffing noise, his breath warm on her lips. “I’ll be fine, Carla. I’m gonna find Rose and I’ll bring her to you. Some friends of mine should be with you sometime tomorrow. You can tell them everything. They’ll come find me, if I’m not back by then.”

“You’d better be back by then!” There were tears running down her face, and she couldn’t stop them.

“Sh.” He kissed her, lightly, fingers tracing under her eyes, wiping away the tears. “I’ll be back, Carla... and when I do, I’m probably gonna need a lawyer, so you better be ready. I’m not in a merciful mood.”

"I should probably be concerned about you going all vigilante.” Her mouth trembled. “But if we’re right... my mother was one of their victims. So don’t be merciful.”

He kissed her, once, a firm press of his lips against hers, and then he was gone, slipping out of the car so quickly and silently, she twitched with shock. The only sound was the very faint click of the door closing behind him. For a brief moment he was a shadow outside the window, and then he was gone into the trees, so utterly that but for the fading warmth on her lips, she might almost wonder if he'd ever been there at all.

Go home, she told herself, taking a deep breath and putting the car back into Drive. She flipped her lights back on as she approached the turn, eyes everywhere looking for a police car, or any other car.

Nothing. All the way to her house. She parked up on the street right under a streetlight, breathing a sigh of relief as she fished out her keys. Go inside, get her own gun from the safe, use her landline to start making calls. Marcus Deveraux from the DA's office first - it was late, but she had his personal number - and then a laundry list of other influential folks.

There were no lights on in her house, of course, but then she hadn't left any on that morning. There wasn't a switch in the hallway, but she'd lived there long enough to know her way around in the dark. She kicked the door shut behind her, hearing the deadlock engage, fumbled for the chain to put on, then walked up the hallway with her fingers lightly brushing the wall until she reached her office door. Pushing it open, she reached for the light switch, but before her questing fingers found it there was a soft click and the lamp on her desk came on, illuminating the room, and the tall figure lounging comfortably in her office chair.

"Evenin', Miss Ramirez," Sheriff McCarthy said equably. "Been waitin' on you."

For an interminable moment, Carla just stared at him. "How did you get in?" she finally said, unable to think of a single other thing to say.

"You rent this house, Miss Ramirez." He gave her an almost pitying look. "Who do you think owns it?"

The name on the lease wasn't Philip Hunter, or Hunter Industries, but no doubt the man had a dozen shell corporations. Carla silently cursed her own stupidity - and swore aloud as she saw the filing cabinet drawer ajar beside the sheriff, the crowbar lying on the floor beside the broken combination lock. The files lying on her desk.

"Those are my confidential client files!"

"Some of them very useful, too." The sheriff didn't even blink. "Woodvale PD thanks you for the information, Miss Ramirez."

"Fuck you!"

He tutted, shaking his head slowly. "Not real ladylike of you, Carla."

His use of her first name shifted something. His attitude changed from calm confidence to something else; an air of leashed menace that terrified her. She tried to order her knocking knees to steady.

"What do you want, Sheriff?"

"Where's Jason Hunter?"

"I have no idea." She said it with complete truth. "He took off."

McCarthy's lip curled. "And left you all alone."

She didn't like the mocking drawl. Wanted to punch that smirk off his face, but knew with painful honesty that she was no match for him physically. All she had was her wits to outsmart him with, but she couldn't even make a dent in that until she knew why he was here and what he wanted.

"I can't help you with Jason Hunter. He's a loose cannon."

"He sure is, but I think we'll have to disagree about what you can do. I think you can definitely help us deal with him, because I reckon I know where he's headed." McCarthy uncoiled from the chair, rising to his feet. "You an' me are gonna take a little trip, Carla."

"I am definitely fucking not!" She wasn't going to win this fight, but she wasn't going down without one. She was pretty sure he wasn't going to shoot her, which meant she might have a chance to get some licks in. Whirling, she made to run, thinking if she could just get to the kitchen, get a knife...

A mule kicked her between the shoulder blades, and she went down to the ground writhing and twitching. Taser, the last rational part of her brain supplied, right before it shut down entirely.

Jason slid silently through the darkness, listening intently as he moved. He'd made a complete circuit of his uncle's property, checking the perimeter. Such as it was, because on one side there was no real boundary. Just the deep woods.

Somehow, Jason didn't think it was because his uncle liked the deer having the opportunity to wander into his back yard.

He'd heard a dog bark once, a deep bay which was clearly coming from somewhere close to the house, though not inside. Not a shepherd breed, he thought. Some sort of pit dog, or a crossbreed. A fighting dog? He knew Philip was casually cruel, might enjoy dog fights. He had the space here to invite friends around to watch them if he wanted; the property was at least sixty acres in size. But an illegal dog fighting ring wasn't what was being protected here. Wasn't big enough to justify all those people disappearing.

There were lights on in the house; not all of them, but several windows, and once or twice Jason saw a shadow move inside the house, knew at least one person was in there.

The question was, was Aunt Rose in there?

He crept closer, listening. If the dog, or dogs, got wind of him they might set up a clamor. Hearing another baying yelp on the other side of the house, he moved closer again, a bit more confidently. He'd approach on this side, see if he couldn't get a look in a window.

The sound of an engine and wheels crunching on gravel had him slipping back into the darkness beside a couple of large trees again. Headlights briefly raked over him, but Jason wasn't worried; he'd smeared dirt on his face to darken it within moments of getting out of Carla's car, was wearing dark clothes and standing still in the shadows. He would be impossible to pick out from a moving car.

A garage door slid up and Jason watched as the car, or rather truck, rolled inside. A new and expensive F150, fully tricked out.

His uncle's? Who was home, then? Philip Hunter had been married, once, but his wife had long since departed for better pastures, licking her wounds and gratefully accepting the pitifully small payout he'd deigned to offer, just relieved to escape.

The door rolled back down and Jason moved from between the trees, crept quietly closer to the house. External lights meant he'd have to cross an exposed patch of ground sooner or later, and he paused to assess the best spot.

There, he thought. Hard to see at that angle from any of the windows. He'd be at the corner of the house, between a lighted window on one side and an unlit one on the other. He didn't see any cameras on the house, which meant he wasn't likely to be observed. Gearing up to dash across the ten-metre gap, he froze as a voice shouted his name.

"Jason!"

Was that his uncle's voice? It was further around the back of the house. He melted back into the trees, moved silently in that direction, careful not to let so much as a single dry twig snap under his foot.

"I know you're out there, Jason!"

No, he doesn't. He's guessing.

There was a balcony on the second floor. Ridiculous, in this climate; there might be a couple of months of the year warm enough to sit out on it, and then if you did you'd be eaten alive by the bugs. He could make out French doors behind it, though no lights. One of them stood open.

Lifting the rifle to his shoulder, he sighted in on that door. Three figures there, he thought, all standing close together, one tall, one medium height, one short.

"You might be thinking your uncle will hesitate to hurt his mother."

That was a different voice. Sheriff McCarthy, Jason thought, focusing on the tallest figure. I was right. That bastard's in this up to his neck.

"I can assure you, I won't hesitate to throw her off this fucking balcony."

Jason would blow his head off before he even got Rose close to the edge of the railing. He adjusted his aim very slightly. Zeroing in on the bastard's head.

"But, Philip would rather I didn't. So I picked up a different piece of insurance. I've got a pair of bolt cutters here, Jason. For every minute that passes until you present yourself at the front door, I'm going to cut off one of sweet Carla's fingers."

Shock froze Jason in place for a long, horrifying moment. Then the three figures shifted, the tallest one moving back slightly, and there was another short one, right in front of him.

"Minute one starts now, Jason. Bring your guns. You left the receipts in Carla's car, so I know exactly what you bought. Leave one behind, you'll cost her a finger."

He started running. He didn't know how many men were inside that house. Even if he shot McCarthy and his uncle, there might be more. Had to be more, considering the sheer number of disappearances. He didn't believe McCarthy was the only dirty cop in the sheriff's department, for one.

He was nearly to the front door when he realized he had one gun McCarthy didn't know about; Rose's little Walther. No time to do anything complicated, but he let his rifle swing on the strap around his neck as he quickly unsnapped the holster off his belt and shoved the gun, holster and all, into a plant pot beside the front door, flicking a handful of dirt over it even as he rapped the knuckles of his other hand on the door.

Chapter Seventeen

"Seventeen seconds to go," his uncle's voice said from somewhere above him; another window, Jason supposed.

"I'm here. Let the women go, Philip. You've got what you wanted."

"Oh, we've got a long way to go before that's true. Put the guns on the ground, Jason. Remember, we know what you've got. Right out there on the driveway, so I can see them. And then take your clothes and boots off and put them down too. I'm sure you've got a knife or two you brought back from Columbia or wherever the fuck it is you've been; let me see those too."

"You're real scared of me, hey, Uncle?" Jason said jeeringly. "I've been waiting a long fucking time for this, you know. For you to show your true colors to the world."

"World ain't watching, kiddo. Let's see those knives."

"Just the two." He held them up, tilting them so they caught the porch light, then tossed them away onto the gravel. "Though I've never needed more than one to kill a man. What's your preference, Uncle? Your preferred victims aren't usually men though, are they? Mostly kids or older folks. Who was your favorite? Those two college girls?"

He stripped off his jacket and shirt, dumped them on the ground. Bent to unlace his boots and step out of them. Unfastening his belt, he shoved his pants down, entirely unselfconscious about stripping off in the chilly autumn darkness.

He had, after all, been through far worse during his Ranger training.

"Leave your shorts on; nobody wants to see your junk," Philip said, as the front door clicked open. It didn't open far; just enough for someone to toss a pair of zip-cuffs out through the gap.

Jason didn't wait to be told, just picked the cuffs up and cinched them on, yanking the one on his left wrist tight first, then using his teeth to secure the right one, both hands in front of him.

If he'd waited, Philip might have ordered whoever was at the door to come out and secure Jason's hands behind his back, and that wouldn't be convenient. Some Rangers Jason knew could get their legs through the loop of their arms when their hands were cuffed behind them; Jason knew he wasn't one of them.

"All right," Philip said when Jason lifted his hands. "Walk to the front door and put your hands above your head against the door."

Pretty dumb if someone was going to open the door, Jason thought, but apparently that wasn't what was going on. Tires crunched on the gravel and headlights lit him up as a car pulled into the driveway.

I know this dude. I remember him from the sheriff's office, that first day. Jason narrowed his eyes. "Deputy Allen, isn't it?" he said dryly. "What a pleasant surprise."

"Shut up." Allen's fist plowed into Jason's short ribs. He barely flinched. The deputy was soft; not ex-military, he was pretty sure. That punch probably hurt Allen's fist more than it did Jason.

"Bring him in," Philip ordered. "Time for a little face-to-face chat with my nephew, before the others get here."

Others? Jason's ears pricked up.

Allen prodded Jason inside, and up the stairs to a great room furnished with more buck antlers than any sane person would ever want to see in a lifetime. The tiger and bearskin rugs on the floor told him everything he needed to know about Philip; his uncle thought he was a mighty hunter. An apex predator.

And suddenly, Jason knew exactly what had happened to all the people who'd gone missing from Woodvale and Redstone Creek and who knew where else, over the last few years.

"Sick little puppy, aren't you?" he said conversationally, eyes taking in everything important in the room. Rose and Carla sat huddled together on a couch. Carla's hands were bound behind her and there was a gag in her mouth. Her hair was disheveled and her eyes spat murderous fire at Sheriff McCarthy, perched casually beside her on the arm of the couch, gun held negligently in his hand. Bolt cutters rested on a table at his elbow, and Jason gritted his teeth at the sight.

Rose was unrestrained; she wasn't wearing a headscarf, the last pitifully thin wisps of her hair shining softly in the light. Tears trickled in a slow, steady stream down each withered cheek, and Jason's heart broke at the sight.

Philip was sitting in a leather armchair, a glass in his hand, amber liquid shining in it. He smiled smugly, gesturing expansively with the glass.

"Take a seat, nephew."

Jason ignored him, walking straight over to the couch and bending down to look into Rose's eyes, ignoring Philip's sputter of fury and the sheriff jumping to his feet.

"You okay, Aunt Rose?" he asked.

"I never dreamed he was this awful," she whispered, her voice thready and weak. "If I'd had any idea... I'd have strangled him in the cradle!"

That was his beloved aunt, still fierce and feisty despite everything. He kissed her brow. "I'll get you out of here," he promised softly, and saw the faith in her eyes. More faith than he had right now, that was certain, but he had to project the confidence for her sake.

"Sit the fuck down." McCarthy cocked his gun ostentatiously.

"Oh shut up. You're not going to shoot me in here. It'd make a mess of Philip's pretty trophy room, and you're so obviously his bitch, he'd make you clean it with your own fucking toothbrush." Jason shot the sheriff a scornful glance, even as he moved a step to the side and reached to release Carla's gag. She spat it out.

"I'm sorry, Jason, he was in my house waiting for me. Tasered me." She shot a black look at the sheriff.

"I'll cut his dick off with those bolt cutters for that," Jason promised, and was rewarded by

Carla laughing, her eyes glittering. She knew they were in a hell of a situation too, he saw. They knew too much. They'd been brought here to die. Rose alone might be spared, for a while at least, depending on just how much feeling Philip had left for his mother.

More car tires were crunching on the gravel outside. McCarthy nodded at Deputy Allen, who left the room quietly, presumably going to pick up Jason's clothes and weapons off the gravel and welcome the new arrivals.

"So." Philip took a sip of his drink.

"You're a shitty host, Philip. Can't even offer your flunky a drunk." Jason needled at McCarthy again, saw the sheriff's face flush. Philip owned McCarthy, but the man didn't like it, that was obvious.

"Shut up, Jason." Philip leaned back in his chair, entirely relaxed, and took another sip. "Now, we can avoid a great deal of unpleasantness if you'll just do one simple thing."

"And that is?"

"Plead guilty to Julia Bulridge's murder, of course."

He laughed, incredulous. "Do you seriously think that would make all this go away? Leave you free to carry on your nasty games without scrutiny? Dream on. Too many people know."

"Are you talking about your journalist friend?" Philip shook his head, affecting a sad expression. "Such a shame about him. Drink-driving is a scourge. Went off a bridge on his way home from work. They didn't find his car yet."

Poor Barry. Jason didn't let his fury show, though. Just cocked his head. "All he did was put a few more victims on the tally for us. The FBI have it all now."

Philip's smile vanished.

"He's bluffing," McCarthy said. "I told you. I've got a buddy in the local field office. He'd warn me if anything had come in. Anything at all."

"Good thing my buddy's in an entirely different field office, isn't it?" Carla put in, her voice falsely bright. "And that we warned them state politics might be involved and the local office might have been put under pressure to look the other way?"

"Shut up, bitch!" McCarthy's face twisted, and he swung his arm back, as though he was about to backhand Carla across the face.

Jason took a fast step forward. "You lay a finger on her, and I'll make you eat your dick after I cut it off!"

Carla couldn't believe what she was seeing. Jason was literally standing there wearing nothing but his shorts, his hands cuffed in front of him, and yet such was the sheer menace he exuded with the threat, McCarthy hesitated.

"Enough!" Philip said, and it was very obvious who was running the show, as McCarthy turned to him deferentially. "If you're not going to take our very reasonable offer, Jason, then I'm afraid you'll have to amuse us in another way. You picking Mrs Bulridge up on the road the other night interrupted our hunt, and I have some disappointed clients because of it. I promised them a good hunt tonight to make up for it."

His smile was nothing short of cruel as he looked his nephew in the eyes. "So, it's up to you, Jason. Who's going to be the hunted?"

He's making him choose, Carla realized sickly.

"Let Carla and Rose go," Jason said evenly, "and I'll give you the hunt of your wildest dreams."

"That's not the deal, boy." Philip sipped his drink again, smirking. "It's just about who dies quick and who dies slow."

"In that case," Rose spoke up, surprising them all, "I'll be the hunted. Since I'm already dying slow."

Philip startled, before setting his glass down. "No. Mom... no." He covered his slight lapse of feeling quickly, though. "I'm afraid you won't provide much challenge for the hounds or entertainment for the hunters. Though Julia Bulridge surprised us, I have to say."

They've been hunting people. With dogs.

It was all suddenly, horribly clear to Carla. She swallowed down bile.

"Don't be stupid," Jason said, speaking slowly, as though to a small child slow to grasp a concept. "If you're just going to kill us all, I have no incentive. Offer me a way out, however unlikely. Tell me that if I survive until dawn, you'll let the women go."

McCarthy laughed. "You've got no idea, have you? Longest anyone's lasted was three hours. And that's after we started giving them a half-hour head start, to give the dogs a challenge."

"Then it costs you nothing to make me the promise. Hell, who can trust a promise given by a scumbag like you anyway? Just tell me that if you haven't killed me by dawn, they get to live too."

"Fine." Philip shrugged. "And if you don't give us a good enough hunt, I'll send Carla out as a secondary prize."

"Deal." Jason nodded, apparently satisfied.

He just convinced Philip to keep us alive for a little while at least, Carla thought. He's got a plan.

She just didn't have any idea what it could possibly be.

"I don't think we'll give you half an hour head start, though," Philip said. "Fifteen minutes should be plenty."

Jason nodded as though completely unsurprised. He looked at Carla then, said quietly "Hang in there. I'll be back for you both."

McCarthy laughed, rising to his feet. "You're an arrogant little shit. Looking forward to letting my dogs chew that out of you."

"Take him downstairs," Philip ordered. "I'll lock these two up and join you. Get him ready."

"He looks plenty ready to me." McCarthy cast a scathing glance over Jason, who still appeared completely unbothered by his near-naked, barefoot state. "Let's go." He reached to put a hand on Jason's shoulder, apparently changed his mind when Jason snapped his head around and shot him a scalding look. McCarthy turned the hand movement into a point instead, gesturing at the door. “That way.”

They were both afraid of Jason, even near-naked and unarmed. His confidence had them rattled, and despite the situation being utterly dire, somehow Carla took strength from that.

She had to believe Jason really did have a plan.

Or she’d start crying and not be able to stop.

With her hands bound behind her, and Rose to worry about, there was nothing Carla could do but obey when Philip told them to leave the room and go down the stairs. She caught a quick glimpse of Jason, standing in a brightly-lit room in the center of a small crowd of men kitted out in hunting gear, before Philip prodded them into a kitchen, opened a door and directed them down another flight of steps.

It was a wine cellar, Carla saw as the light snapped on. A pretty fancy one, with temperature-controlled cabinets lining one wall and a rustic wooden bench in the middle of the room, six chairs around it.

"You'll be safe down here until the time comes," Philip said. "I don't even mind if you want to share a bottle of wine. Enjoy your last night." He looked at Rose, seemed about to say something else, but she turned her back on him, and he went back up the stairs without another word. The door at the top closed with a heavy thud, and Carla heard the metallic snap of a key turning.

For about thirty seconds she and Rose stood in silence, staring at each other, and then Rose exploded into motion. "We need to get you out of those cuffs." She reached under the bench, pulled open a drawer and pawed through it. "Thank goodness the little shit didn't turn the light off. There's got to be something sharp in here..." she opened another drawer. "What kind of wine cellar doesn't have a fucking corkscrew in it?"

Carla almost laughed at the unexpected curse from the old lady. "Break a glass." She nodded towards a glass-fronted cabinet against the wall, full of sparkling crystal glasses. "Or a wine bottle, whatever. Just don't cut yourself."

Rose yanked the cabinet door open, selected a glass and carried it over to the sink in the corner. Tapping it on the metal edge, she grunted as it shattered. "Bits are too small. Let's try another one."

She seemed satisfied with a shard she produced on her second try, beckoned Carla over.

"Wrap the edges in one of these napkins." Carla nodded at the pile of napkins in one of the drawers. "Seriously, Rose, we don't need to add your bleeding fingers to our troubles right now."

"You better just hope I don't manage to accidentally slit your wrists, young lady." Rose's voice trembled.

"I'm quite sure you won't." Carla fought to project the same calm, unshakeable confidence Jason had upstairs.

"Hm." Edges of the shard safely wrapped, Rose moved behind her. "Brace your hands on the corner of the table, will you?"

It took surprisingly little time for the flex cuffs to part, at least on one wrist, and Carla didn't care about the other. She took the glass shard from Rose's hand when Rose would have attempted to cut the other one off. "It doesn't matter. I'll cut it off once we're out of here. Let me take a look around."

She raced back up the steps on light feet, pressed her ear against the door. They'd been hearing booted feet clomping around, but the sound had stopped a couple of minutes ago, while Rose was working on the cuff.

"Has it been fifteen minutes?" Rose's voice cracked.

"No, but I doubt they'd give him fifteen," Carla said honestly. "They're scared of what he can do. They'll tell him fifteen and give him ten. Or five."

"Lying, cheating little bastard." Rose said down heavily in one of the chairs at the table, buried her face in her hands. "I didn't know. I swear, Carla, I had no idea..."

"I know." She came back down the stairs. The door wasn't going to open without a key, a key she didn't have, and it was the only way out.

The only thing she could do now was comfort and take care of Rose, as best she could.

Although.

She eyed the cabinets.

She might grab a couple of bottles and have them ready to hand. If whoever came down those steps wasn't fully alert, she might just be able to brain him with one.

"What's expensive?" Rose lifted her head as Carla opened a wine cabinet. "Something nice, but with a screw top..."

"Isn't that an oxymoron?"

"Honestly, it's been so long since I had a glass of wine I couldn't tell the good stuff from rotgut anyway. A glass of red, if you please."

Philip did have expensive taste in wine, Carla realized, as she looked at a few labels. With a shrug, she selected a screw top bottle, cracked it open and poured a glass for Rose. "You might want to let that breathe a minute... or not," as Rose picked up the glass and drained half of it.

“Keep it coming,” Rose said, setting the glass back down. She smiled wryly at Carla’s shocked expression. “I just found out my only son’s a sociopathic serial killer, Carla, apparently heading up some ghastly sort of human sacrifice hunting cult. This is highly likely to be my last night on earth. Forgive me for wanting to drink myself into a coma.”

“Jason’s coming back for us,” Carla said stoutly. “You’ll need to be able to walk out of here under your own steam.”

Rose just looked at her, lifting the glass to her lips and taking another mouthful. “Well,” she said after putting the glass down again. “If he does… if we get to walk up those steps… you might be able to use this.”

Carla gaped at the mobile phone Rose slid out of her sleeve and placed on the table. “Where the bloody hell did that come from?” she gasped.

“Picked Philip’s pocket. Arrogant idiot.” Rose shook her head, reaching for the wine bottle. “There’s barely any signal in this part of town anyway, and there’ll be none in this cellar. At best, you might get an emergency call out…

and if you think it's not one of McCarthy's own on the dispatch line tonight, I have a bridge in Brooklyn to sell you."

"Rose!" Carla grabbed the phone. "There might not be phone reception, but Philip probably has WiFi!" Please don't be face or fingerprint locked... she turned the phone on with shaking fingers. It was an older model Android; apparently Philip wasn't all that technologically minded. A grid of dots appeared on the screen. She'd have to replicate a pattern on them. Holding the phone up to the light, she tilted it, squinting. There. A greasy shape on the screen... a squared-off letter P.

Praying desperately, she traced her finger over the line. And, unbelievably, the phone unlocked, presenting a screen full of familiar icons. And a Wifi icon at the top with four bright curved lines.

She might not have much time. If Philip realized his phone was gone, if he suspected for a moment Rose had filched it, he'd be back down here in a second. Even if he just switched the WiFi off, they were screwed. She thought frantically, even as she opened up her usual video conferencing app, logged out of Philip's account and into her own.

"Please, please pick up," she muttered, scrolling her contacts. "Please be working late, Marcus. Please."

"You're lucky I'm working late," Assistant District Attorney Marcus Devereaux said. "Suze has taken the kids to her sister's for a movie night..." he looked up at his screen finally, obviously saw Carla's dishevelment, and blinked. "What the hell..."

"I might not have much time, so please listen," Carla said quickly. "Marcus, Rose Hunter and I are locked in a wine cellar in the basement of Philip Hunter's house. I was abducted from my house by Sheriff McCarthy, who Tasered me and brought me here... so clearly not a legal arrest by any stretch of the imagination. Not only that, but they're running some kind of weird human hunting ring, and they've forced Jason Hunter to go out in the woods... they're hunting him down. With dogs."

"Jesus Christ," Marcus said, but she could see from his expression that he believed every word.

"We don't know how many people from the local sheriff's department are in on it, but Redstone Creek is compromised too. Journalist Barry Hillsum met with us earlier; he's got notes on almost fifty people who've disappeared between the two towns. Or he did. Philip told us they've disappeared him too. Car went into a creek on his way home from work."

"FBI?" Marcus said.

"Has to be, doesn't it?"

"Stay on this call, Carla. I'm recording it now. I'm going to start making calls, but keep talking. Let's get as much as possible on record."

Carla knew what he wasn't saying. In case the FBI didn't get to her in time. Even by helicopter, it would be forty minutes at least, and that was once Marcus got them moving.

This might be her dying statement, and Rose's too. So she marshaled herself and began to speak, laying out everything she knew or suspected. Getting it all on the record… just in case she didn't live to stand up in court and give a witness statement.

All the while, wondering if Jason was still alive.

Chapter Eighteen

"So, this is how it's going to go," McCarthy drawled. He stood in the center of a loose semi-circle of men. "You got ten minutes to run like a scared fuckin' rabbit. Meantime, I'm giving those clothes to the dogs, so they get a nice load of your scent."

"I'm sure Philip said fifteen minutes." Jason looked him hard in the eye.

"Fine. Fifteen." McCarthy smirked, and Jason knew he'd be lucky to get a full ten. Lifting his arm, he glanced at his watch. "You're already thirty seconds in. Better start running."

Jason didn't wait. Satisfying though it would have been to punch McCarthy in the mouth before he started running, there were seven men in that semicircle including his uncle, watching him, every one of them with a hunting rifle in hand. He spun on his heel and ran hell-for-leather for the tree line.

Without boots, his feet weren't going to hold up all that long on the rough ground.

Fortunately, they didn't need to.

He ran in as straight a line as he could figure, as fast as he could, for four minutes, dodging around trees he could barely see in the poor light. It wasn't going to be a four-minute-mile by any stretch of the imagination, but because of the thick tree cover he'd be far out of range of even their night scopes by the time he made a hard left turn and ran for Greens Road, retracing his steps from what couldn't even be an hour ago but felt like days.

He was sprinting hard back along the road, able to see his footing intermittently in the splashes of light coming from the houses on the far side, when he heard the first deep bay from the dogs.

He was counting on the handlers - McCarthy and whoever else worked directly with the dogs - not letting them off leash. Which meant the dogs could only go as fast as the humans with them could run. Not as fast as Jason Hunter, who'd been the fastest runner in his Ranger regiment and hadn't let his running regime slacken off in the slightest since he retired to his semi-civilian life training anti-narcotics paramilitary personnel in Guàlize, he was betting.

And that meant that by the time the dogs found the spot where he'd made his sharp left turn, Jason was running up the drive to his uncle's house, sweating and breathing hard, feet burning with pain... but knowing he had at least five minutes in hand, and that was if someone turned around and came straight back.

He was hoping nobody had stayed behind to guard Carla and Rose. He'd heard Philip state his intention to lock them up, though, seen from the corner of his eye Philip opening a door under the stairs and pushing the two women through it.

Jason paused briefly by the front door to retrieve Rose's handgun from the planter pot, before sprinting back around to the back of the house. The front door was too heavy for him to kick in, as was the back door he'd seen, and he didn't particularly want to make a lot of noise smashing a window.

It took him only seconds to scale the side of the house up to the rear balcony, and, incredibly, although the French doors had been closed, they weren't locked. With an incredulous shake of his head, Jason slipped inside and ran for the stairs.

He was tempted, so tempted, to take a minute to look for his weapons. Or any other weapons. He did pause five seconds in the kitchen to yank a knife from the rack and cut off his flex cuffs; while he'd done fine thus far with his hands cuffed together, he still much preferred to have them free. He kept the knife. It was an expensive Japanese one, nicely balanced. Might be handy.

The key was in the lock of the door under the stairs. He opened it quietly, listening. The house had been utterly still and silent so far, but now he could hear a woman's voice, filtering faintly up the stairs.

"Carla?" he called quietly.

There was a brief pause. "Jason?"

She sounded incredulous. He grinned quietly to himself. “Can you come up here? I don’t want to get locked in down there with you, if they come back.”

“How the… no, save it. I’m on a call with the FBI. You can explain it to them.”

“On a call with the FBI?” He couldn’t believe it. How had she managed that?

Rose came up the stairs first, hanging on to the rail at the side, looking more frail then ever. Carla was right behind her, a phone in her hand.

“You’ve still got my gun,” Rose said as she came up to him, a weak smile creasing her face.

“It was the only one they didn’t know I had. Hid it and picked it up when I came back. Hurry. We might not have a lot of time.”

Rose still came in for a hug. Jason grinned despite his worry, holding his arms wide so neither knife nor gun was anywhere near her. “I’m sweaty, Aunt Rose. Been running.”

“You’re the most beautiful sight I’ve ever seen.” The hug was tight, despite her weakness. “Can we leave now?”

“Bad idea, I’m afraid. I presume reinforcements are on the way?” Jason said, raising his eyebrows at the women looking at him out of the tiny screen in Carla’s hand.

“Helicopters lifting off as we speak,” the woman said. “We scrambled HRT. About forty minutes to wait.”

“We’ve got five minutes max, probably less, before they realize I’m back here. Even if we get lucky and the keys are still in one of the cars in the drive, I doubt we can outrun all of them. I might not know all their names, but I’ve seen all their faces, so they have to kill me. My uncle and McCarthy are done, but some of the others might be able to go back undercover… as long as I’m not around.”

“So we, what, wait for them to come to us?” Carla gulped.

“They’re not going to come in fat and stupid. McCarthy knows what I’m capable of. None of them were carrying two rifles, which means the one I brought is here somewhere. We have to find it."

"I don't think they brought them upstairs." Carla caught on fast, looking around.

They split up and hurried through the downstairs rooms of the house. It was Rose who found the weapons, in Philip's study, lying on his desk. "In here!" she shouted, and by the time they got to her, she was sitting in Philip's desk chair, the pump-action shotgun laid across her lap. "This one will do me nicely, darlings."

"I was going to suggest we lock you in the cellar, hide the key, and tell Agent Carruthers where her people can find the key," Jason said dryly. The FBI agent still on the video call was hiding her mouth with her hand, obviously stifling laughter, aware it was an inappropriate moment to laugh when the three of them were in serious danger.

"Fuck that," Rose said eloquently. "Is that a brandy decanter? Bring it here. If I'm going out tonight, I'm going out in style, and hopefully I'll take my godawful son with me. Did you hear that, Agent?" she called towards the phone in Carla's hand. "If any one of those bastards is killed tonight, I did it."

"I'll make a note of that, Mrs Hunter," the agent said gravely.

Jason offered Carla the pistol silently. She paused, but then took it from his hand. Her fingers were quivering, she was obviously terrified, but he could see that she was also mad as hell.

His shirt and pants were gone - given to the dogs as McCarthy had said, he supposed, but his combat vest and boots were lying in a messy pile on the floor. Dragging the vest on, Jason shook his head as he found his spare clips still in the pockets. His combat knife was even in one boot.

Carla was opening desk drawers as he pulled his boots on and tied a rough knot, not bothering to lace them properly. She made a triumphant sound and held up another gun, a .45 from the look of it. Too big for her tiny hand, she offered it to Jason; he checked it quickly, finding a magazine full and another in the chamber. He nodded at Carla and tucked it into a vest pocket.

In the distance, he heard a dog baying.

"Here they come."

They'd been turning off the interior lights as they moved through the house, Rose directing Jason to the switches which controlled the outside ones. Outside, the place was lit up like a Christmas tree, but inside, it was dark and quiet. Jason switched off the light in the study now, gestured Carla and Rose to get down low to the floor, below the level of the windows.

"Careful with the light from the phone," he said quietly. "Switch the camera to the rear one, and hold the screen against your body so the light doesn't show."

"Tell them the FBI are on the way, Lieutenant Hunter," Carruthers said. "Some of them may back down and make a run for it. We'll get them, of course, but it'll leave you a few less to deal with."

"Sure," Jason said dryly.

They all knew that the hunters, whoever they were, needed to eliminate witnesses. No witnesses, no evidence, would make even the video evidence the FBI now had - which Philip and his minions weren't aware of - potentially vulnerable. Especially if Philip Hunter had friends in high enough places.

Inconveniently alive witnesses weren't nearly as easy to make disappear.

"The dogs are getting close." Carla sucked in a ragged breath, looking at Jason. He'd pressed them to get down, below window level. Rose had tucked herself in under Philip's desk with the brandy decanter and the shotgun; she had a clear view from there towards the door of the study, and Jason seemed quite happy to leave her a clear field there. He and Carla crouched below the windows, taking it in turns to peek over the sill and look out.

With the outside flooded with light, they had a great view, and the returning hunters were unable to use the advantage their night-vision goggles would give them.

At least, until some of them thought to shoot out the floodlights, Carla thought gloomily.

"Movement," Jason said quietly. The study was in a corner of the house, and he'd put himself by the window which faced the drive, assuming that, if the dog handlers had followed his scent all the way, that was where they'd come.

"The dogs?"

"Yep." Jason had his rifle at his shoulder, looking through the scope. "Two of them. Big beasts; Rottweilers, I think, or Dobermanns, or some crossbreed. They're straining at the harnesses. I think that's McCarthy got one of them, and Allen on the other. They're holding the dogs back from coming into the lighted area."

Carla could imagine what McCarthy might be thinking. They hadn't left the lights on when they left the house, which meant Jason had gotten inside, and then what? Had he taken a vehicle and left? He would have to consult with everyone who'd left their cars in front of the house to figure out if any were missing.

“Shoot the dogs,” Carruthers said from the phone in Carla’s hand, startling all of them.

“Excuse me?” Even in the darkness, Jason looked shocked.

“They’ve been trained to be manhunters, and very possibly, man-killers. There is absolutely no way we’re going to do anything with those dogs but have them put down immediately. Shoot them now. Before McCarthy lets them loose in the house with you and you have a problem.”

Jason clearly thought about it, looking through his scope, then back at Carla. She saw his jaw tighten, then he gave her a half-smile.

A moment later, the rifle boomed, shockingly loud in the exposed space. Jason had opened the bay window just far enough to shoot through, so there was no shattering of glass.

“Damn,” Jason said, tone conversational. “I missed. I hit one of the handlers, not the dog.”

Carla covered her mouth to keep from laughing. She was absolutely certain Jason had, in fact, hit exactly what he was aiming at.

"Looks like I got him in the leg. Now there are several people crowding around, dragging him away. Sorry, Agent Carruthers, I don't have any clear shots at the dogs right now."

If he'd admitted to deliberately shooting one of the hunters, before they fired, he might be in trouble, Carla thought. But an 'accidental' hit, when Carruthers herself had given the order for him to shoot the dogs… that was absolutely brilliant, and took at least one of their opponents off the field, probably more than one. Someone would have to look after the injured man, after all, and someone else would have to take the dog, possibly someone who wasn't used to handling it.

"Do you think you got McCarthy?" she asked softly.

"No. He was behind the other dog," Jason said, and Carla understood. Allen, or whoever was the second dog handler, had been the only viable target.

"Are they in earshot? Tell them we're coming. Hell, shout FBI; put down your weapons!" Carruthers said.

“FBI!” Jason dutifully shouted out the open window. “Put down your weapons and walk into the light with your hands above your head!”

It’s worth a try, Carla thought.

“Fuck off!” a roar came from outside. McCarthy, and he sounded pissed. “Ain’t no FBI here!”

“Not yet, but they’re on their way!” Jason called back. “HRT, so you know they’re coming in loaded for bear. Not Rangers, but I’ll be happy enough to see them anyway!”

There was silence, for a couple of minutes. And then Carla heard something. A creak.

“Jason,” she hissed. “I think that was a door opening.”

He nodded, holding a hand up in a clenched fist, in a signal she recognized from enough movies; be quiet and be still. He pointed at his window, beckoned to her. She crept across as quietly as she could.

“I’ll go check it out,” Jason breathed into her ear when she was next to him. He put the night-vision goggles down in front of her foot. “If the lights go out, use those.” His cheek brushed hers lightly, his lips caressed fleetingly across her forehead, and then he was slipping away, pausing by the desk.

“I’ll call out before I come back, Aunt Rose. Anyone else who comes through that door before the FBI arrive, blow them to kingdom come.”

“You got it,” Rose promised, gripping the shotgun fiercely.

There was another creak, closer now. Someone outside in the hallway.

Carla held her breath.

Jason lowered his rifle. Slung it around to his back on its strap, and pulled the .45 Carla had found in the desk out of his pocket. Finger resting on the trigger guard, he reached for the door handle, and in a move so fluid and swift Carla could barely follow, he jerked the door open, rolled through it and was gone.

There was the deep boom of a rifle. The flat crack of the .45, once, twice. The excited bark of the dog; Jason said “Oh, fuck,” and then there was crashing and banging, more gunshots, a pained scream and then, a horrible, tense, singing silence.

“Jason?” Aunt Rose’s voice quavered. “Jason, are you there?”

Chapter Nineteen

Leaving Carla and Rose alone was the last thing Jason wanted to do, but staying put and waiting for the hunters to kick the door in and spray the room with bullets was also not an option. He was going to have to go out there and cut the head off the snake. And he needed to do it quickly and hope while he was gone, someone else didn't come in through the windows.

Rolling out into the hallway, he stayed low, fully intent on shooting the kneecaps off anyone he found. Killing them would create more trouble with the FBI than he really wanted, especially considering the powerful friends and relatives some of these folk obviously had, but he had no compunctions about hurting them badly enough to make sure they were out of the fight.

The bullet hit the wall just above his shoulder. Too close range, Jason thought, seeing the shadow in the doorway at the end of the hall; he aimed the .45 and fired off a single shot.

There was a scream of pain and the shadow staggered backwards. Someone else swore, a dog barked, and somebody shouted “Let it go!”

The scrabble of claws on hardwood was the only warning he had before the dog was on him, all snarls and hot breath and snapping teeth. Jason rolled with the impact, twisting away from those vicious jaws before the dog could get a grip on him, shoving the muzzle of the .45 into its belly and pulling the trigger.

“Oh, fuck!” he said in disgust as blood sprayed over his hands and the dog fell away with an agonized whimper. He hadn’t wanted to kill the dog, had hoped to avoid it, but knew Agent Carruthers was right; dogs trained to hunt and kill humans were too dangerous for even the most fervent of animal lovers to try and save.

"Jupiter!" It was McCarthy's voice. "Jupiter, come!"

Jason didn't bother to let McCarthy know the dog wouldn't be coming. Just rose silently to his feet and moved, one slow, silent step at a time.

"Jupiter!" McCarthy shouted again. "Come here, you fucking stupid beast!"

One more step, and in the light flooding in from one of the outside lights, Jason made out Deputy Allen, writhing on the floor, clutching at his leg. Shot in the thigh. From the amount of blood, Jason hadn't hit the artery; Allen would live, as long as he got medical attention. He'd already got a pad of cloth over the wound and his belt cinched tight around it, so Jason had no compunction about hitting him hard over the head with the pistol butt when Allen tried to shout a warning.

A dog whined, close. Just around the corner in front of him, Jason thought.

"Minerva," McCarthy said, quietly, "hunt."

A leash snapped. Claws scrabbled. The dog burst around the corner, just building up speed, and Jason made it quick, a double tap straight into her gaping jaws, before stepping around the corner and finding himself face to face with the sheriff.

McCarthy was caught off-guard, startled by Jason being so close. He still had the dog's leash in his right hand, his sidearm holstered at his waist, a semi-automatic rifle dangling across his body on a sling but his hand nowhere near the trigger. Jason appearing in his night-vision right on top of him, gun aimed at his face, must have been a shock, but he reacted quickly, jumping forward and grabbing Jason's hand, pushing it out to one side to get the barrel pointing away from him.

It was fine with Jason. He didn't want to kill McCarthy. He stepped in closer himself and kicked McCarthy hard in the knee.

The sheriff buckled with a yell of agony, letting go of Jason's hand as he clutched instinctively at his knee, and Jason followed up with an elbow strike that shattered his nose.

McCarthy was writhing with pain, but still had enough presence of mind to try and grab for his weapons.

“Don’t be a dick.” Jason disarmed him with easy efficiency, checking the semi-automatic and claiming it for himself. Not trusting McCarthy not to do anything stupid, he dislocated both his thumbs with a couple of powerful wrenches at his hands. “Now.” He pointed the gun between McCarthy’s eyes. “I’d prefer to leave you alive for the FBI, but they’re already aware that you’re a serial killer, so I don’t think they’ll cry too hard if I have to kill you. Who else came in the house apart from you, Allen and the dogs?”

McCarthy’s mouth tightened mulishly.

Jason sighed and stepped on his dislocated left thumb.

McCarthy’s scream echoed off the walls.

“Who. Else. Is. In…”

“Your uncle!” McCarthy was panting with agony. “The others ran for it, fucking cowards. Got in their cars and ran home. Left us to clean up.”

“There’s no cleaning this up.” Jason could hear Aunt Rose calling his name. “Hold tight, I’ll be right there,” he called back reassuringly.

Carla sagged with relief as she heard Jason call back to them, his voice calm and steady. She’d looked over her shoulder to the door instinctively, turned back to the window now, scanning outside.

All the lights went out at once, and Carla flinched, grabbing for the night vision goggles on the floor. She shoved the phone in her shirt pocket so she could keep her other hand on the gun, holding the goggles up to her eyes and peering out into the now green-tinted dark.

“Carla?” Rose quavered.

“They’ve shut off the power,” Carla said shortly. “Fuze box in the garage, probably. Keep watching that door, Rose. You’ll hear their footsteps if anyone comes up to it; it’s a wooden floor, and Jason won't come up to it without telling you."

"Can you see anything out there?"

"No." They all had night vision, Carla thought; they had the advantage now. And Jason didn't. "Jason!" she hissed loudly. "Goggles!"

Silence. Then, shockingly close, a click. Carla whirled, shocked, but a door, a door which had been hidden by a bookcase, was opening almost on top of where she was crouched on the floor, and a strong hand grabbed her gun hand before she could even bring it up.

She screamed instinctively, then again in pain as the gun was twisted away and her index finger broke in the trigger guard. The goggles clattered to the floor, and a hand closed on her throat, dragging her to her feet and back against a solid male form.

"Scream again, little bitch," Philip Hunter rasped in her ear. "Let my nephew know you need him."

"Let her go!" Rose struggled out from under the desk, getting slowly to her feet, brandishing the shotgun.

“Rose, no!” Carla panted. “Don’t shoot!” With a shotgun, at this range the only thing Rose could do was fill them both full of lead, and Carla was in front.

“Put it down, Mother,” Philip sneered.

“I will bloody not!” Rose’s finger was outside the trigger guard, though, the barrel swinging away. Pointing back at the door. “If any of your friends come through that door, Philip, I will blow them to kingdom come.”

“Clearly, you’ve lost your marbles, mother dear.” Philip sounded quite calm. “Such a shame. You’re going to be found out in the woods, dead of exposure, having wandered off.”

“The fuck?” Carla said, stunned.

“Jason lost his mind with worry. Stormed over here, broke in, accused me of some terrible things. I was having a quiet evening playing cards with friends. Miss Ramirez here, she’s a great poker player... but she was killed in the crossfire as we tried to defend ourselves.”

“That’s quite a narrative you’re crafting there,” Carla said acidly, “and it might even work, if your buddy Sheriff McCarthy was the one investigating it all. Since you're even now on a live call with Agent Carruthers of the FBI, though, I don't think it's going to fly."

Philip went rigid. She felt cold steel at her temple as he pressed Rose's pistol harder against her face. "You're lying. McCarthy searched you; you didn't have a phone on you when he picked you up!"

"It's your phone, dickhead. Rose stole it out of your pocket earlier, and you left your WiFi on. We've been talking to the FBI since two minutes after you locked the cellar door. The Hostage Rescue Team will be here in a matter of minutes. Phone's right there on the windowsill; pick it up if you don't believe me."

She felt him half-turn away from her. Something hard on his leg brushed against her little finger, and she wracked her brain, trying to think what it might be. How he had looked when he spoke to them earlier. There'd been something strapped to his leg. Was it a hunting knife? Delicately, she eased her fingers back an inch, trying to ignore the agonizing throb in her broken index finger.

Crashes and thumps, punctuated by the occasional gunshot, sounded outside the study, but Carla couldn't think about anything but what was happening right here and now.

"Pick up the phone, Philip," she taunted. "Say hi to Agent Carruthers."

"Looking forward to speaking with you in person, Mr Hunter," Carruthers' voice said dryly from the phone, a little tinny and muffled because the phone was face down on the windowsill. "Shouldn't be long now. So I suggest you let Ms. Ramirez go, put down your weapons and go outside. Face down on the ground with your arms above your head will definitely be the best pose to choose if you'd like to peacefully surrender yourself."

"Fucking bitch!" Philip yelled, and the gun left her temple, before a shattering bang left her blinking and temporarily deafened.

He'd shot the phone.

And he too must be temporarily stunned by the noise: Carla twisted like she was trying to get away, clawing at his hand on her throat with her left hand, even while her right jerked at the snaps on the leather strap holding the hunting knife in its sheath, clumsy because her index finger just didn't work.

"Let her go, Philip."

It was Jason's voice, just outside the study door. "I'm coming in, Aunt Rose. Don't worry about the others. I dealt with them."

"Yes," Philip growled, shaking Carla like a dog with a rat. "Get in here."

He was turned on, Carla realized, suddenly sickened; she could feel his arousal inside his pants, prodding at her lower back. There was something very, very wrong with Philip Hunter.

There was barely any light. Just the slightest shift of a shadow in the doorway, no sound at all. The gun barrel moved away from Carla's head again, and she knew with sudden, absolute clarity that Philip Hunter was going to shoot Jason. Philip knew he was going down, and the only thing he still wanted was to make sure Jason died first.

The leather strap popped and Carla yanked the hunting knife from its sheath on Philip's thigh, folded her fingers around it, ignoring the screaming spike of agony from her broken finger, and stabbed it back as hard as she could into the muscle of his thigh.

Philip yelled, the gun went off, but she thought the shot was wild, aiming at the ceiling. He let go of her throat and she flung herself away from him, letting go of the knife, her hand slippery with blood as she crashed to the floor. Her head banged against the base of the heavy wooden desk.

Dimly, as though from a great distance away, she heard Rose scream, heard Jason shout her name.

And then blackness descended.

For a sickening moment, Jason thought Philip had hit Carla with that single wild shot. But he couldn't have; Jason had felt the bullet whiz past just over the top of his head. Carla was down, though, and so was Philip, falling back yelling abuse as he clutched at his leg.

Jason leaped across the room, covering the distance between them in a couple of rapid strides as Philip tried to lift his gun with shaking hands. One kick and it went spinning away.

In the night vision goggles he'd taken from McCarthy, Jason could see the knife sticking out of Philip's thigh. The blood pulsing fast out of the wound as his uncle sagged limply.

Carla had hit the femoral artery. Even if Jason tried, he doubted he could stop the bleeding, or even slow it enough for Philip to have a fighting chance of survival by the time paramedics could get there.

Frankly, he didn't care. He was more than happy to let Philip bleed to death.

Rose was kneeling beside Carla, feeling frantically over her in the darkness, calling her name. Jason spun to crouch beside her, cursing when he saw the awkward angle she was lying at.

"I think she hit her head on the desk. Don't move her, Aunt Rose!" He felt at her head, her neck. Her pulse was beating strongly, her breathing steady. “She’s alive but she might have hurt her neck. We’ll wait for help.”

“Jason.” Rose’s voice was thin and thready. “I… I’m so sorry. I didn’t know… didn’t know he was…”

“How could you?” he said gently, reaching to put his arm around her shoulders. “It’s over. I promise. It’s all over now.”

They stayed like that, crouched on the study floor over Carla’s unconscious body, Rose sobbing against Jason’s shoulder while Philip’s blood pooled around his slowly cooling body, until the sound of helicopter blades overhead signaled the arrival of the FBI.

Chapter Twenty

A steady beeping sound brought Carla slowly out of slumber. A bright light overhead made her squint when she blinked her eyes open, and she closed them again quickly with a disgruntled hiss.

“Carla?” a voice said quietly. There was something familiar about it, but she couldn’t immediately place the speaker.

“Lights,” she grumbled. “Who’s that?”

“It’s Marcus, Marcus Devereaux. Just a moment.”

She heard him get up from the chair beside the bed, move across the room. Click a switch.

“Try that.”

She opened her eyes a mere crack, relieved to find the glare was gone. Turned her head to look at Marcus and had to swallow a scream as agony stabbed at her.

“Don’t move!” He rushed back to the bed, leaning over her. “You have a hairline skull fracture and a lump on your head the size of a tennis ball.”

Her throat was dry. “Jason,” she croaked. “Rose?”

Marcus’ face was grim, and for a horrible moment she thought he was going to tell her Jason hadn’t made it. That Philip Hunter had managed to get the last laugh, had killed the nephew he hated so intensely.

“Rose isn’t good. Jason’s with her. You’re in the hospital, Carla... in Seattle. The FBI wanted you out of state while they rounded up everyone in the hunting ring. Airlifted you and Rose here.”

“How long?” Carla’s head was starting to pound. A nurse came in; Marcus must have pressed a call button when she woke up, Carla registered.

"You've been here four days. They've kept you asleep because of the swelling on your brain. Carla." Marcus leaned in even as the nurse flashed a penlight in Carla's pupils. "You did it, Carla. Philip Hunter's dead and the FBI rounded all the rest of them up. They found a bone pit in Philip's back yard..."

"Mr Devereaux, you need to leave," the nurse told him briskly. A doctor came hurrying in too. Carla could hear the speed of the beeps increasing; it must be measuring her pulse, she registered dimly. She wanted to ask about the bone pit. Wanted to ask about her mother, but Marcus was allowing himself to be hustled out and the nurse was fiddling with something on the IV tree, coolness flooding her blood.

Her eyes drifted closed.

She woke an indeterminate mount of time later, the pain in her head a little less agonizing when she cautiously moved it. It was night, she thought; the room dim and shadowed. Agent Carruthers was sitting by the bed, reading a report.

"Agent," Carla croaked out.

“My name’s Sarah.” Carruthers’ eyes crinkled at the corners as she picked up a cup from the nightstand, brought a straw to Carla’s lips. “I think you’ve earned the right to call me that, Carla. How’s that head feeling?”

“Sore.”

“Understandable. I’m not going to ask you any questions just now - Jason Hunter and Barry Hillsum have filled us in on everything they know - but when you’re ready, we’ll definitely want to hear anything additional you can tell us.”

“Barry?” Carla’s eyes widened.

“Ah yes, your journalist friend turned out to be harder to kill than Philip Hunter and his buddies thought. Turns out he was something of a champion swimmer back in your school days, I understand? Managed to get out of his car when a logging truck pushed him off a bridge into the river, swam to safety.” Carruthers smiled, obviously amused. “He’s been on all the news channels, the face of the story, since you and Jason aren’t available. Sold several articles to the New York Times, I believe.”

Carla couldn't believe it. Barry too had survived. She closed her eyes in relief, feeling a tear leak out between them. Too many hadn't.

"The bones," she whispered, unable to look at Carruthers. "Mom?"

"We don't know yet. Jason told us to look for her, and we took a sample of your DNA for comparison, but there are a lot of bones, Carla. We have a whole team of forensic pathologists on it, but we've found eighty-two skulls. It's a lot."

Eighty-two skulls means at least that many victims, Carla thought. Dear God.

"Thanks to Barry Hillsum, we have a lot of names and we're working on sourcing DNA of relatives so we can identify them, but it's going to take a while. I promise we'll let you know immediately if we find your mom."

Eighty-two. The tears were sliding faster down Carla's cheeks. She gulped down a sob.

"Easy." Agent Carruthers took her hand, a firm, steadying grasp. "It's horrific, Carla, but it's over. You stopped it. A lot of families are going to get closure now, and a lot of folks will be very grateful to you for killing Philip Hunter."

Carla's eyes flew open. "Me?"

"Oh." Carruthers bit her lip, obviously kicking herself for accidentally letting that out. "He bled to death after you stabbed him. But don't you dare feel even one second of guilt about it; if anyone deserved to die, it was Philip Hunter! He started this, you know; recruited Sheriff McCarthy later. One of the victims we've identified vanished two years before McCarthy came to Woodvale. You were still in high school when Philip started killing. They're calling his horrible crew of psychopaths The Manhunters. You stopped one of the worst serial killers in American history, Carla, one the FBI hadn't the slightest clue was out there. You're a heroine."

Lassitude was creeping up on Carla again. She vaguely managed to mutter "Being a heroine seems to come with serious drawbacks," before sleep claimed her again.

The next time she woke up, she felt clearer. It was daylight, the room bright, but the light no longer hurt her eyes, and when she moved her head experimentally, the pain was little more than a twinge. Carefully, she turned to look at the chair by the bed.

Jason was sprawled there, legs stretched out in front of him and crossed at the ankles, head tipped back against the wall. His lips were slightly parted and the sound of slow, heavy breathing told her he was asleep.

Carla just lay there and watched him for a while. There was thick stubble under his jaw, dark circles under his eyes, and his clothes didn't look as though they fit him quite right, as if someone had bought them without actually knowing his size. The sweatpants were too long, the T-shirt too tight across his shoulders, short sleeves squeezing his thick biceps. He looked exhausted, mildly grubby, and he was the most beautiful man Carla had ever seen.

He was still there when she woke up the next time, lured awake by the scent of bacon.

"Is that a bacon and egg sandwich?" she mumbled, squinting at the half-eaten roll in Jason's hand.

"Carla!" He almost dropped it in shock, before bolting to his feet and leaning over her. "You're awake!"

She reached up a hand, pleased to note it didn't tremble, touched his cheek. "Why are you here?"

He frowned, obviously puzzled.

"Rose?"

Jason closed his eyes, shaking his head slowly, and Carla knew.

"Oh Jason. I'm so sorry."

"She knew when she called me home that her time was short," he said quietly. "She was ready. I wasn't."

"I'm so sorry," Carla said again, knowing it was entirely inadequate, as tears welled in her eyes, matching the ones trickling slowly down Jason's face. "She was so unbelievably brave." In the face of discovering her own son was a monster, Rose had never backed down. Had stolen the phone from Philip's pocket, enabling Carla to contact Marcus and call in the FBI. Sat on that study floor with the shotgun in her lap, fully prepared to use it.

Her courage had stiffened Carla's own spine, lent her the determination she'd needed to fight back and stab Philip.

"She asked me to thank you." Jason took a deep breath, scrubbed briefly at his face. "For 'taking care of the Philip problem and saving us all a lot of trouble' as she put it."

Carla couldn't even begin to imagine how Rose must have felt saying that. How awful to feel grateful to someone for killing your child. In a way, Carla was grateful Rose hadn't lived to face the aftermath; the families of serial killers rarely fared well at the hands of the media. No doubt there would be ghoulish types eager to dig into Philip's background and analyze what had turned him into a remorseless murderer, and some would point the finger of blame at Rose.

Jason was crying, unashamedly, and Carla reached towards his face instinctively. He buried his head in the bedclothes at her side, and she stroked his head and neck tenderly as he slept, a small, selfish thought creeping in to her mind.

He'll be leaving now.

There was nothing left for Jason in Woodvale but awful memories and the notoriety of being Philip Hunter's closest living relative. He'd surely be departing for Guàlize as soon as possible, probably right after seeing to Rose's funeral arrangements, desperate to shake Woodvale's dust from his boots for the last time.

And Carla would never see him again.

Even though she'd only known him a matter of days, grief gripped her heart at the thought. Jason Hunter was charming, sexy... and probably the bravest man she'd ever met. He would be very, very easy to fall in love with, but she wouldn't get that opportunity.

A nurse came breezing in just then, smiling to see Carla awake. Jason pulled back, wiping at his eyes. "Out you go, Mr. Hunter," the nurse said amiably, "we're just going to need a little privacy for a few minutes."

It turned out there were some quite unsexy things to deal with after having been unconscious in a hospital bed for the best part of a week, and Carla wasn't too sorry Jason had been shooed out. Once the nurse had finished, a doctor came in to examine her, checking the lump on her head, shining a light in her eyes and more, and once she had left, Agent Carruthers came in.

From the look on her face, Carla knew what Carruthers was coming to tell her. "Mom?" she asked, choking up.

"I'm so sorry, Carla, but yes. We have DNA results on several bones which are a first-degree female match to yours."

She'd already known, Carla tried to tell herself, but it didn't help. Not when she thought of what her mother's final hours must have been like. An agonized wail welled up in her throat, the cry of a wounded animal, and then Jason was there, holding her close, and she sobbed against his chest until exhaustion -- or maybe the painkillers being pumped into her IV -- claimed her again.

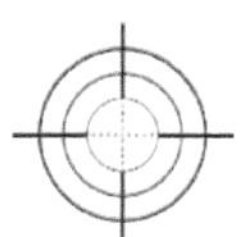

Jason waited until Carla was entirely limp before laying her back down on the pillows, pulling the sheet over her chest and collapsing to sit back down with a groan. It was only then he noticed that the FBI agent hadn't left; Carruthers was propping up the wall on the other side of the private hospital room.

"Heard your aunt has already been cremated," Carruthers said.

"It was what she wanted," Jason said bleakly. "She was very clear about her wishes. Said she wanted to stay with me, not be scattered and forgotten and definitely not buried in Woodvale. The hospital have the facilities; a local funeral home brought me a nice urn." It was in his hotel room, a room the FBI had arranged for him but he'd barely spent more than a few minutes in. Every hour had been spent with Rose, until she passed, or here at Carla's bedside, waiting for her to awaken.

Carruthers nodded. "It'll be a while before we can release Mrs. Ramirez's remains, I'm afraid. We have to test every bone, work out which belongs to what victim."

Jason shuddered at the thought. With so many bones, the FBI had to prioritize; they'd taken a tooth from each of the eighty-two skulls found in the bone pit and DNA tested them first. Now came the painstaking work to test and identify which victim every single bone belonged to before the remains could be returned to their grieving families. No doubt there would be dozens of others receiving the same news Carla had, today and in the days to come. Some who might not even be aware their loved ones were even missing, from what Barry had told them.

"I need to tell you something," Carruthers said abruptly. "And I'm not sure how you're going to take it."

"I've never been the sort to smash things when life doesn't go my way," Jason said wryly. "Hit me with it."

"We found Philip Hunter's will when we searched his property. Seems like he had some small amount of conscience left towards his mother. If he predeceased her - which considering her diagnosis, he obviously didn't expect - she inherited his entire estate."

Jason blinked. "I beg your pardon?"

Carruthers gave a sharp little nod. “And I understand you are your aunt’s primary beneficiary. Which obviously, she thought was just her house and personal effects. But it’s not... you’re going to inherit all of Hunter Industries, the logging concern, the properties, and every other piece of pie Philip Hunter had his fingers in.”

He didn’t know what to say. He didn’t know what to think. The only thing he felt was an instinctive revulsion. He didn’t want anything that had been Philip’s, even though a small voice in the back of his head - a voice which sounded suspiciously like Rose’s - was pointing out dryly that by rights, half of it should have been his all along, his rightful inheritance his father was cheated of.

“Compensation,” was what came out of his mouth. “The families of victims. They should get the money.”

Carruthers cracked a smile, and it reached her eyes, crinkling them up at the corners. “I knew you were a good sort. I think you’re right. I’m sure you could put it all in a trust or something. A good lawyer would be able to help you set it up." She cut her eyes meaningfully at Carla.

"She'd be entitled to a share herself. Her mother," Jason clarified.

"Of course; I wasn't thinking. Still, I'm sure she could advise you on the best way to go about things. Or that DA friend of hers might be able to recommend someone. Devereaux." She nodded sharply and pushed herself off the wall, unfolding her arms. "Whatever you decide to do, it's been a pleasure."

"You're leaving?" Jason asked as he shook her offered hand.

"Called back to D.C. I'm afraid. There's an inconceivable amount of paperwork in a case like this. I'll be buried in the bowels of the Hoover Building for a while." She didn't look displeased about it, and Jason suspected there might be a promotion in her future over her handling of the case. She was the one Marcus Devereaux had called when Carla got hold of him from Philip's wine cellar, had listened and taken them seriously, pushed the panic button to get the Hostage Rescue team rolling.

“Thank you for everything.”

“Good luck,” was Carruthers’ parting comment, before she nodded her head and slipped quietly out of the room, leaving Jason alone with the sound of Carla’s steady breathing.

He wasn’t alone for long. Marcus Devereaux arrived, nodding to him before taking a seat beside him.

“How’s Carla doing today?”

“Pretty good. She was awake and talking a little while ago. Carruthers broke the news that they identified her mother’s remains.”

Marcus winced. “Ouch.”

“She was pretty upset. The nurse told me earlier that the swelling on her head is almost gone, though, and the MRI they did yesterday shows no internal swelling at all. She’ll be good to go home in a couple days, though she’ll have to take it easy for a while.”

“Have you met Carla?” Marcus chuckled lightly. “I don’t think ‘take it easy’ is in her skillset.”

Jason laughed too, before sobering. He glanced sideways at Marcus, before deciding to trust him. He'd certainly earned it. "Carruthers also told me that due to Philip predeceasing my aunt Rose and a complicated provision with his will, I'm going to inherit his estate. Which I very much do not want."

Marcus pursed his lips in a silent whistle. "I can see why, but he must have been worth millions. You'd never need to work again."

Jason raised an eyebrow. "Have you met me?" He echoed Marcus' words of a few moments ago, making the DA laugh.

"Well, we haven't known each other long, but I can see you're not the kind of guy who would do well sitting idle. Which was something I wanted to talk to you about, actually."

Jason raised his eyebrows.

"Because I might have a job offer for you."

Chapter Twenty-One

Ten days later

Carla stared out the window of Marcus' car, watching the trees go by, thinning out as they entered Woodvale. The town looked just as it always did; somehow she'd thought it would seem different somehow, after everything that had happened. The sheer normality of it seemed almost obscene.

The FBI still hadn't identified every bone -- it might be months, she'd been told gently, and it was also very certain that nobody was getting back a complete skeleton. Too many bones were missing. The total count of victims had gone up to eighty-five, three more being found through the DNA testing, whose skulls hadn't been present in the bone pit. Carla shied away from thinking about what had happened to all those missing bones.

She'd forgotten about the mess in her office until she walked in, and then she was surprised to see that it had been cleaned up. Not only that, but her whole house was sparkling clean, and when she opened her refrigerator, suddenly wondering if there was green milk in there, even that was clean and sweet-smelling, and filled with fresh groceries.

"Who did this?" she asked Marcus, who was leaning against the kitchen door watching her with an amused expression.

"The day after you were airlifted to hospital, four quietly charming but slightly terrifying Guàlizeans turned up. Made themselves useful all over the place; defused not a few situations around the town which were getting pretty sticky in the absence of a sheriff's department."

Carla nodded in sudden understanding. The entire department had been arrested and questioned by the FBI, and though only Allen and McCarthy were confirmed to have been involved with the Manhunters, the rest were still on suspension pending investigation. State police had been sent in to manage day to day issues, but there must have been a couple of days at least of near-chaos.

“And the Guàlizeans cleaned up in here?” She looked back in the fridge again.

“Fitted new locks to your doors, too.” Marcus handed over a ring of keys. “Your car tires look suspiciously new, as well.”

“Who needs a fairy godmother or house elves?” Carla smiled, hoping she’d get to meet her mysterious benefactors one day, though she was sure they’d already gone home by now.

Marcus took his leave a few minutes later, and Carla made herself a cup of coffee and got out some cheese and crackers to eat, not feeling able just then to put together anything more substantial. She’d make a meal later. Maybe. She still tired more easily than she liked.

A knock on the door made her sigh and push herself wearily to her feet. It might be Barry; he'd said he wanted to stop by. He was planning to write a book on the story, already had interest from several major publishers, and had asked Carla to consider being a co-author. Considering the size of the advances that were already being offered - and the fact that Netflix had also called him - she was seriously considering it. Even a small share would set her up for life.

Swinging the door open, she froze for an instant at the sight of a sheriff's star, flinching back instinctively as memories of finding McCarthy sitting in her office came rushing back. Her eyes traveled up and her mouth dropped open.

"Hey," Jason said with a warm grin.

"Wh-what. How. Why are you wearing that uniform?" she finally managed to gasp out.

"Turns out Woodvale needed a sheriff in a hurry." He leaned on the doorframe and lifted one shoulder in an eloquent shrug. "I'll need to get elected if I'm gonna stay on, but the acting mayor appointed me on a temporary basis."

“The acting mayor… oh.” Carla remembered. The mayor was one of Philip’s cronies who had been arrested along with the rest of the Manhunters. The deputy mayor, a woman Carla had never met, had obviously stepped up, recognized that in Jason she had a potential solution to a major problem, and convinced him to stay on and help out for a while.

“Things are a bit complicated,” Jason understated, “but I need to stick around for a while anyway. Turns out it’s more difficult than you’d think to give away a large fortune to the families of a serial killer’s victims.”

Carla nodded. She could only imagine.

“And, funny thing. With my uncle gone… Woodvale’s pretty nice. I was thinking I might stay long-term. Town needs a sheriff.”

A spark of hope began to dawn in Carla’s heart. She stared at him, not sure what to say. Hardly believing it might be real.

“I realized something else, as well.”

“Yeah?” Carla almost breathed it.

“Little bird told me you have a fridge full of ingredients… and I never did cook you that dinner I promised you.” That wicked dimple appeared in his chin as he grinned crookedly at her.

“Later,” Carla said, reaching out to grab him by the front of his shirt, pulling him into the house and kicking the door shut behind them. “You can cook me dinner… later.”

Epilogue

Six months later

Dressed in formal, funereal black, Carla stepped forward and laid the bunch of spring wildflowers on the plinth. An angel of white marble, wings cupped protectively, stood atop it, and into the plinth eighty names had been carefully chiseled... with space for six more as yet unidentified victims of the Manhunters.

The statue was in the grounds of Philip's former house, now bulldozed and removed without trace, a lovingly tended garden springing up in its place. Today was a special memorial service, families of the victims coming together to dedicate the garden to the memories of their loved ones.

Jason stood silently, at a distance. He was the one who had made all this possible, insisting that the house and grounds must not be sold, deeding the property to the town and doing a good deal of the work to start the garden himself, in his off hours.

He'd been elected as sheriff unopposed, and had begun building a team of reliable deputies, several of them former Rangers, all of whom were currently busy enforcing the media perimeter for this ceremony. Woodvale had been absolutely overrun with journalists and would-be true crime aficionados since before Carla had gotten out of hospital, and they showed no sign of losing interest in the story. The only exception to the media ban at the memorial service was Barry Hillsum, who had sold his book rights for a seven-figure advance and was currently conducting a series of sensitive and moving interviews with the families of the victims. Determined to make the story about the victims rather than the killers, he was trusted by all the families to report sensitively on the memorial service.

Carla wasn't surprised when Jason stepped up, after all the family members had paid their respects, and laid his own offering of flowers at the base of the plinth. He touched the letters spelling out the name of Julia Bulridge, the Manhunters' last victim, the only one they knew for sure hadn't been buried in the bone pit as her body had been left in Rose's garden to try and frame Jason.

Carla knew Jason would always feel guilt over Julia's death. He still wondered aloud sometimes what would have happened if he'd managed to get her back to town alive. Personally, Carla thought that McCarthy would have killed both Julia and Jason immediately, in fear of the secret being exposed, and who knew how many more might have died for the Manhunters' twisted entertainment.

Jason straightened, and came to Carla's side. She slipped her hand into his and smiled up at him, aware that telephoto lenses were probably clicking away at this small, intimate moment. Both of them were more than slightly horrified by the celebrity status the media seemed to think they deserved, but they refused to pretend they weren't together. The Netflix producer charged with bringing the story to the screen had been absolutely delighted to have a romance to add in, and had even asked if they were getting married. Jason's death stare had made the man back down, fortunately.

"You doing okay?" Jason asked quietly, and Carla nodded, fingers tightening around his. "Let's get out of here, then."

His deputies kept the media firmly at bay as they got into Jason's car and drove away, heading for Rose's house. Carla hadn't felt quite safe in hers, ever since McCarthy's invasion, so they'd moved into Rose's house together. Some days, Carla could swear she felt Rose's presence there, happy and benevolent, watching over them.

It would be a beautiful home to raise a family. Carla rested a hand over her stomach, a secretive little smile coming to her face. She and Jason hadn't always been as careful as maybe they should, but she wouldn't regret it.

She planned to tell him, tonight. She'd wanted to wait until after the memorial service.

"I wanted to wait until after the memorial service," Jason began, as they sat side by side on the old porch swing on Rose's back porch, watching the sunset over the forested hills, "to ask..."

"I'm pregnant," Carla cut him off, grinning at his shocked expression.

"Then I guess it's even more important," he said, after getting over his initial surprise, "that I ask if you'd consider making this a permanent arrangement." Fishing in his shirt pocket, he pulled out a ring. "And not only that, but I wanted to ask if you'd consider allowing me to take your name."

It was Carla's turn to be astounded, but she nodded in dawning understanding. "There've been enough Hunters in Woodvale?"

"Too many."

She smiled at him, reaching to take the ring and slip it onto her own hand, holding it up to admire the flashes of light reflecting from the simple but stunning square-cut diamond.

"Yes, to both questions. I'll marry you, and you can dump being a Hunter. Forever."

He put his arm around her shoulders and leaned over to kiss her, soft and tender, which quickly turned hot and passionate, until she stood, laughing, and took his hand to tow him into the house.

The screen door slammed shut, their laughter fading as they ran though the house together, leaving only the sound of the wind whispering gently through the trees behind them.

THE END

The Rescue Rangers will return in Ranger's ission, when injured Ranger Drew Murphy takes up Jason's offer of a job with the Woodvale sheriff's department, but is asked to take on an undercover assignment before putting on the uniform. An assignment that will end with Drew fighting for his life... and that of the feisty ATF agent who might be his only chance of survival.

If you enjoyed reading Ranger's omecoming, please consider leaving a review on Amazon, Goodreads or Bookbub, and thank you for taking the time to read!

You can find my web page at caitlynlynch.com. Pay a visit and sign up to my mailing list to be notified of my next scorching hot publication! I also share regular giveaways, tell you about super freebies and new releases from author friends of mine.

(You can unsubscribe at any time, and I promise not to spam you.)

Also By Caitlyn Lynch

RESCUE RANGERS SERIES

RANGER'S RESCUE

RANGER'S HOMECOMING

RANGER'S MISSION

RANGER'S BLOOD

SUNFISH ISLAND RESORT SERIES

FINDING CORY

THE RELUCTANT BILLIONAIRE

HER FAKE ISLAND WEDDING

SLOW SIMMER

FIGHTING FATE

CROP IT LIKE IT'S HOT

STANDALONE BOOKS

IF WISHES WERE HORSES - AN IRISH ROMANCE

CAR CRASH LOVE

KITTENS FOR CHRISTMAS

DANA'S DUO

HOT FOR HEATHER

ELEVATOR ENCOUNTERS SERIES

ELLIE'S ENCOUNTER

JULIET'S ROMEO

THE BEST MAN FOR LEAH

RANGER HEAT SERIES

FIRST SUBMISSION

SECOND SURRENDER

THIRD THRILLS

www.ingramcontent.com/pod-product-compliance
Lightning Source LLC
Chambersburg PA
CBHW020946310726
48980CB00001B/76

* 9 7 8 0 6 4 5 1 8 2 8 7 3 *